TOTTE

# TOTTER'S TEAPOT

Gordon Savage

MILESTONE PUBLICATIONS

Published by Milestone Publications
Murray Road, Horndean, Hampshire PO8 9JL.

**British Library Cataloguing in Publication Data**

Savage, Gordon
Totter's teapot.
I. Title
823'.914[F] PR6069.A93/

ISBN 0-903852-62-4

Typeset by Inforum Ltd, Portsmouth
Printed and bound in Great Britain by
R.J. Acford, Chichester

# The Teapots

# Illustrations

# Acknowledgements

To David Tallis I am indebted. Descendant of the composer, one time big drummer and miracle worker with musical boxes, it was he who gave me my first sight of Bunhill Row from Armoury House and access to Honourable Artillery Company records.

My thanks are also due to Sally Ward without whom the first manuscript would never have been typed.

The following have been kind enough to help with the illustrations for which many thanks, Judith Miller of Millers Price Guide, Philip Broadbridge, Secretary of the London and Provincial Antique Dealers Association, Sam Twining O.B.E., of Twinings, Captain Newberry of Parker Gallery, The Guildhall Library and Museum, Frances Raymakers of A.D.C. Heritage, Leslie Weller of Sotheby's King & Chasemore and Brian Eldridge

To Barbara, my wife,
and
Marika, Jill and Luanne,
my daughters

# Foreword

Every antique dealer worth his salt will have known the urge which prompted this book. We buy and we sell, often before fully observing what has passed through our hands. We are in business and our livelihood depends either upon our margins or the speed and magnitude of our turnover.

And in the course of our business we learn. There are human angles. The widow parts with a family treasure to pay for her son's schooling. A clergyman gets dispensation to sell an ancient chalice so that the roof of his church may be repaired. A family painting must go to pay the taxes.

All these things have a history. They didn't just happen. Someone made them, created them to meet a need or a whim, perhaps painted them to satisfy an irresistible urge. Someone paid for them. They had a context and a background of day-to-day happenings.

I chose a Hester Bateman teapot for my story.

A man told me once he didn't like silver because it was boring. He said it was all the same colour. Shortly afterwards I visited the Silver Vaults in Chancery Lane and I understood what he meant.

There were rows of similar looking shops, each set solidly in a huge safe. One had the sensation of entering a series of refrigerators and wondered if the thing worked like the light in the one at home. Open the door and the light goes on, the scenario inside just rolls, and the cases of candelabra, teapots, salvers and salt-cellars, start to pour onto the markets of the world.

It isn't really like that at all. I went round later with an enthusiast. The candelabra became relics of the retreat from Moscow. A salver had belonged to a rather naughty Peer. A teapot was made by Hester Bateman. Colour is in the eye of the beholder.

I once owned a good Hester Bateman pot. As a very tentative, struggling young dealer, I bought it out of a huge pile of pieces which a famous saleroom representative had rejected as worthless. Because the big boy, who must surely know so much more than I, had rejected it I sold it too cheaply, but not before I had learned the date of its manufacture, 1782.

Later I discovered that the Royal George went down off Spithead in that year with the loss of Admiral Kempenfeld and some eight hundred ordinary people, hands, officers and their families. it just wasn't done to swim in those days. Even Lord Nelson never acquired a skill considered bad for the health. There was no dramatic action. The ship was alongside the docks and with so many souls aboard the middle gunports were opened to the fresh air. One source has it that the weight of the rum ration for the next voyage, being loaded at the time, was sufficient to bring the ports below water level and cause the ship to keel over. Now there's a story Hester Bateman, an intelligent woman of her day, must have heard about and discussed, just as she must have seen, even met, Vincente Lunardi. Wouldn't you watch if someone turned up in the street outside your house with a great red and blue airship?

There was no William Fibb, but there was a Lieutenant Shipp who published an account of his military exploits initially to draw attention to the vicious field punishments meted out to the ordinary soldier in the early nineteenth century. In the event he quarrelled with a fellow officer over the purchase of a racehorse and his literary effort only supplied a small addition to his pension. To his history much is owed. He certainly drank tea, and there's a great deal of Shipp in our orphan from Paxham.

He-Sing's mode of arrival in England was a mystery to me until I discovered a folder in which Mr Lambert kept all the papers commemorating a day out in the London docks with his son, George. The Chinaman's likeness appears with that of Queen Victoria and her entourage in a painting of the opening of the Great Exhibition in Hyde Park in 1851. Melissa and Alice? There must have been at least one woman in Mr Lambert's life since he had a son. A journalist has dubbed Brixton "a land of daughters". One piece of gratuitous information cannot fit the story. The Ke-Ying was eventually bought by a Liverpudlian speculator and broken up. The timbers were used, according to a friendly librarian, to deck the Birkenhead Ferry. Some researcher may choose to discover if they're still afloat!

There was a whole cross-section of society on the Titanic, and there must have been an almost village atmosphere about the suburbs lying close to London. The motor car was still a rarity in 1900.

Older readers will remember the opening days of Hitler's war. I served in it and met my wife over a telephone concentrator. In an Officers' Mess in Germany at the end of it, I listened to Election Results which foreboded the downfall of Churchill, and an elderly Brigadier looked me intensely in the eye. "Our heads are in the tumbril, boy," he said. But we are still here!

The machinations and manoeuvrings of the saleroom are always rumoured but never recorded. Most reputable dealers these days dislike the Ring and have nothing to do with it. A bad auctioneer is its greatest stimulus. Why teach an ignoramus his business? Whatever happens to a teapot, a human agency is involved. There's always a question of "right" or "wrong" when a fairly valuable object fails to accord, in all respects, with accepted convention.

A friend who was kind enough to go through my manuscript "in the rough", persevered, but criticized the abrupt changes of scene.

Shakespeare called the world a stage. People walk on and off playing their parts. When the curtain falls on an episode – exeunt all. The rest of the action is left to your imagination.

Follow a series of plays in one theatre. If you're very observant you may notice some prop appearing again and again. You see it on the eighteenth century pier cabinet, on the Victorian credenza, and next week, there it will be again on the twentieth century mantelpiece. That is the way of my teapot.

So take a look at your treasures. Because they are worth money the tax man may take them before they have told their story.

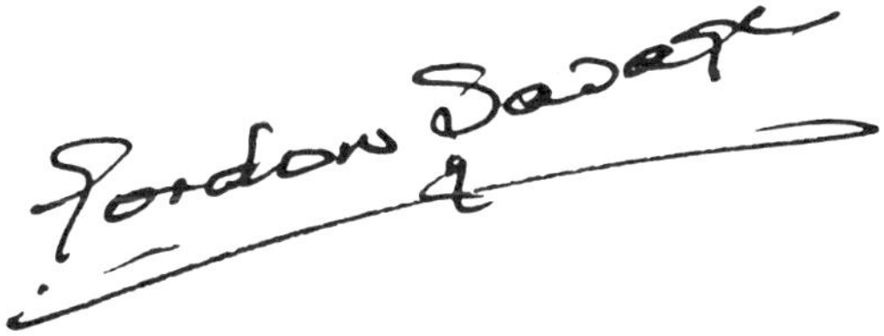

# Bateman Teapot

Number 107 Bunhill Row, a stone's throw to the north of London's ancient civic boundary, had an air of prosperous and active stability. The panelled door and the woodwork were freshly painted, and the heavy, plain brass knocker and finger plate gleamed in the morning light. The arched skylight above it, unlike those on some adjacent dwellings, was relieved of the sooty encrustation from a million belching chimneys and gloried in crisp leaded symmetry. A trick of light appeared for an instant to give it sight like an amiable cyclops. Then a passing scrap of cloud animated the other panes above and to either side. The house looked out upon the vibrant street. Freshly watered greenery thrived in two large troughs and the front, right across the cobbles, had been newly washed down and swept.

Such a house should shelter a merchant of some substance, a wholesaler with a warehouse down by the crowded docks, perhaps a prosperous mercer or even a grocer. One might have expected, if one had chosen to wait and watch for the door to open, the emergence of a tall, resolute figure in a beaver hat, or a rotund, over-indulged trader with a head full of stock returns, certainly a businessman of sorts.

The door did open; it opened suddenly, jarring heavily against the jamb. No imposing merchant stood, however, in the opening. Hester Bateman emerged purposefully at the top of her three freshly scrubbed front steps.

"I want to come with you, Granny". It was a child's voice, not fretful but assertive.

"Jonathan!" The voice floated up from the nether distance. "Come here at once and leave Granny alone."

"Do as your mother says, Jonathan," said Hester indulgently, "or we shall both have to answer for it. Besides, I've things to do." She gently pushed the small, clamouring figure back into the passage and firmly shut the door. She carried under her arm a large, black painted, flat metal box.

Hester's mind lingered in the workshop behind the house. For a moment, and moments tend to linger when one is old, she still relished the dull tympany of beaten metal, the hum and clack of foot-operated polishing wheels, the rasp of a silver-saw; those were the sounds of her life. There were the childish noises too, of course. The breathless farewell of two great-grandchildren was stimulating.

Hester thought briefly upon family responsibility, looking up with some pride at the immaculate front of number 107, quite an achievement. If you were a good parent your offspring should monopolise your whole being. She had built a factory as well. You produced the children and nursed them, then they were yours to care for and feed, to teach and advise, and if possible to direct with the benefit of your own experience. In spite of all the turmoil and heartache, unless they approved your example, which, in the nature of things was unlikely, they went their own way in the end. If they followed you, there surely was a compliment, a favourable gesture from a Fate not always kind.

Extend the generations to the grandchildren and great-grandchildren and the case was different. There was no responsibility then. Other people's children, if they weren't too boisterous, were pure pleasure, particularly when one was advanced in years and sometimes, as one was only too conscious, regarded as an embarrassment. Not that anything was ever said openly. Nevertheless, it was good to have Jonathan's affection – yes, a fourth Jonathan, born three years since – strange if he too became a silversmith. Jonathan was energetic to say the least, into everything, but he was a fine, healthy lad, a favourite with Hester.

The old lady returned to the present with an inward smile at her own vagary. She straightened her sober grey bonnet and smoothed the prim stiffness of her skirt before turning towards the bustle which marked the boundary of London City.

Behind her, up the road where the cobbles gave way to beaten earth, toward the fields beyond the burial ground where John Bunyan lay long asleep, other women went about their affairs with baskets for market, wooden buckets for the pump or heads full of gossip. Most of those who passed bobbed a quick curtsy, but Hester's acknowledgement of the compliments was brief. She had little time for domestic trivialities, particularly other people's, when business called.

It was eight-thirty in the morning and the milkmaids with their yokes had already passed back to their farms. Street vendors cried their fish and meat. Most of the men who lived in Bunhill Row, apart from those who also worked there, had already departed for the City, but those who lingered doffed their hats respectfully to the small old lady with the firm step and clear eye. Even the Serjeant, in a respite from drilling recruits on

*The Honourable Artillery Company at practice. October 1823.*

the Artillery Ground gave her a salute as she passed on her way to visit her banker.

The journey was a familiar one. She had made it as a young matron on behalf of her husband John. In those days, when their small workshop produced mainly chains and small outwork for other smiths, she had carried mostly copper. Much later, when John had died and she had made her own mark, she continued to deposit the ever-increasing harvest of coin, often gold now, bills, notes of hand. In the year 1784 the House of Bateman flourished as a manufactory in its own right. Hester was 73 and this was a significant journey.

She turned left into Chiswell Street, along the south side of the Artillery Ground, paused briefly to appreciate the shining crested carriage with the restless pair of chestnuts held by a liveried coachman, and entered the offices of Mr Jacob Prothero, Merchant Banker, at the sign of the Sea-Horse. A tall, elegant personage doffed his hat as he passed out into the street. "Mistress Bateman."

"Mr Whitbread," said she, in friendly acknowledgement, warmly conscious of acceptance as a colleague in affairs.

The clerk at the high desk, brown wizened and worn, as shiny at the edges as his furniture, emerged like a cheerful, if obsequious chameleon from the gloom and hurried to the counter.

"A pleasure to see you, Ma'am, a pleasure indeed. May I be of . . . er . . . hassistance? Mr Prothero is engaged with Lord Clayburne. Estate affairs, you know. They take a little time, but His Lordship has been here for half an hour already."

At that moment, a door at the far end of the dingy but glinting oak-clad chamber opened to reveal the banker himself, resplendent in long velvet coat above satin breeches. Dark, piercing eyes glowed in pendulous

*The sign of the Sea-Horse perpetuated on a modern bank.*

features, and a Central European origin bequeathed the faintest of lisps.

"Mr Tuttle. I expect Mistress Bateman to call this morning; better let me have a note of the manufactory account. And there's that little matter Her Ladyship discussed the other morning, you remember, when we spoke of the plate for Clayburne. Ah, yes. I'll present her to His Lordship."

The immaculately-tailored, restless little figure marked each syllable with a gesture. The elegant, snowy lace at his wrists was constantly agitated. Steel-rimmed spectacles, worn to impress, unfortunately concentrated the dark eyes to a range of very few yards. Jacob, with his glasses, had been known to confuse his best client, Mr Whitbread of the flourishing brewery, with a neighbour's porter of similar build. Realising that Mr Tuttle was not on his stool he peered, still gesturing, at the counter, and there, finally located and focused upon Hester.

"Ah, Mistress Bateman – your most obedient servant, Ma'am. So good of you to call. I trust all goes well at the manufactory?"

The banker now contrived to lift the counter flap and seize his client's hand in a simultaneous flurry of lace. Hester felt herself swept forward.

"Before we proceed to business, Ma'am, may I introduce you to my most esteemed client?" Jacob turned, removed his spectacles, flourished a ruffle, coughed for effect, and beamed. Introductions meant business.

"My Lord, this is the very lady of whom we spoke. Not at all what either of you expected, I'm sure."

"I am honoured, My Lord," said Hester, eyes a-twinkle, finding herself once again in a familiar situation. "I wonder what you expected. The practice of a craft by the . . . er . . . gentle sex offends you? I believe that times will change. Adam came before Eve, but if she had had something to occupy her mind the serpent could have become apprentice instead of tempter and history would have been different. Master Price, the vicar, he tells me that's sacrilege. But I am an old woman, Sir, and I digress. Mr Prothero has not brought us together to exchange frivolous banter. I know him too well!"

Lord Clayburne would have protested, but Hester raised her hand.

"Let me come to the point, Lord Clayburne. I saw your carriage outside. Our mutual friend my neighbour, Sir James Esdaile, has already told me that you wish to order a service of tea pieces for Her Ladyship. I am no longer young. I take little part in the making of our silver nowadays, but one of my sons, or even the best of the apprentices will make you the finest service you could desire. If it is made in Bunhill Row, Sir, it will be good, and it will bear my mark."

His Lordship had a humorous twinkle in his eye. Living in an age of men, he was hardly accustomed to such direct address from a woman. "Ma'am," he said, as Mr Prothero cast his eyes heavenward, "your – hm – forthrightness does you credit. 'Tis true I spoke to Sir James about the silver. He warned me, too, of you opinions, and acquainted me with your professed retirement. But the fact is, Ma'am, that I find myself in a quandary. Lady Clayburne has set her heart upon something from your own hand – something like this. You understand, she also has very forceful ideas upon the destiny of the ill-fated Eve!"

Lord Clayburne had drawn from his pocket a folded paper which he now spread upon the table. While the banker gazed in astonishment Hester got up and looked over his shoulder.

"Like this, you see, Ma'am," Lord Clayburne said. "No sharp corners, yet not entirely round, and with the beeding and the bright-cutting which so becomes your designs here – and here, with jug to match, so, and the sugar-box like the pot only smaller and without spout or handle. When my wife set this down she said you would know all about the proper finials to finish."

Hester traced the drawing with a forefinger. "Lady Clayburne drew this?"

"Indeed Ma'am. A commendable effort, do you not think?"

"Very commendable indeed Sir." Hester paused. "Her Ladyship would make a silversmith!"

Hester paused again while the two men watched, the banker wringing his hands, Lord Clayburne with a quizzical smile.

"I cannot bear the sight of you both so on tenterhooks," she said, laughing. " 'Twould be an exercise of skill." Hester was savouring the moment. "I'll do it Milord. Give me – shall we say, a month? Upon my word. I'll make the whole thing myself!"

When Lord Clayburne, to the accompaniment of assurances of good-will, had been seen to his carriage by Mr Prothero, and the coachman, who was fresh from the country, had been minutely instructed by Tuttle how to reach Twinings in the Strand, where the best tea from China was to be bought, the banker returned to his desk. There he sat regarding Hester, breathing deeply as if he has just sprinted a hundred yards. Between these two, down the years, had grown up a bond which was almost affection.

"Hester," he said at last, with difficulty. "I do not know how you keep your clients. To speak so to Lord Clayburne! Yet he seemed to be pleased! And you will make him his service? The day of miracles is come.again! How often I ask you to make such a thing for me and always you have said No. And I am your friend!"

"Jacob," replied the old lady, smiling reminiscently. "The teapot for you could never come from Bunhill Row. Your teapot would have to weigh heavier than a basket of potatoes, be smothered in curlicues and swirls and carry the mark of the Lord High Treasurer himself. You would not like my simple lines. Something from France would suit you better, Jacob. Better buy your silver service from somebody else and let us remain friends!"

The two old people looked at each other in silence. Speculation, memories of long ago. For a moment words were superfluous. Then the banker spoke with unaccustomed feeling.

"Yes, Hester, we remain friends. After all these years who would want to change? But it is not for friendship that you come here. What is the business that brings you? Money you have enough. At your time of life you should be sitting before your fire with the children and the grand-children to wait upon you. Veh – but who am I to speak? I too, have no need to sit here counting my money." The old man paused.

"Such a pretty little girl, Hester." The eloquent hands sketched a child. "My father and mother and me, just arrived from Russia. We were tired, dirty – we were filthy and hungry. It was you, Hester who brought us food at the back door of the inn when we had no money to pay." He shook his head slowly from side to side. "We had no English to thank the barmaid! Heh," the whole tragi-comedy of the ghetto breathed into the aspirates – "but much water has flowed since then; it's more than sixty years. And here you come to see me again, half a century from my father's money-changing table. You bring papers. I see dreams in your eyes. What will you

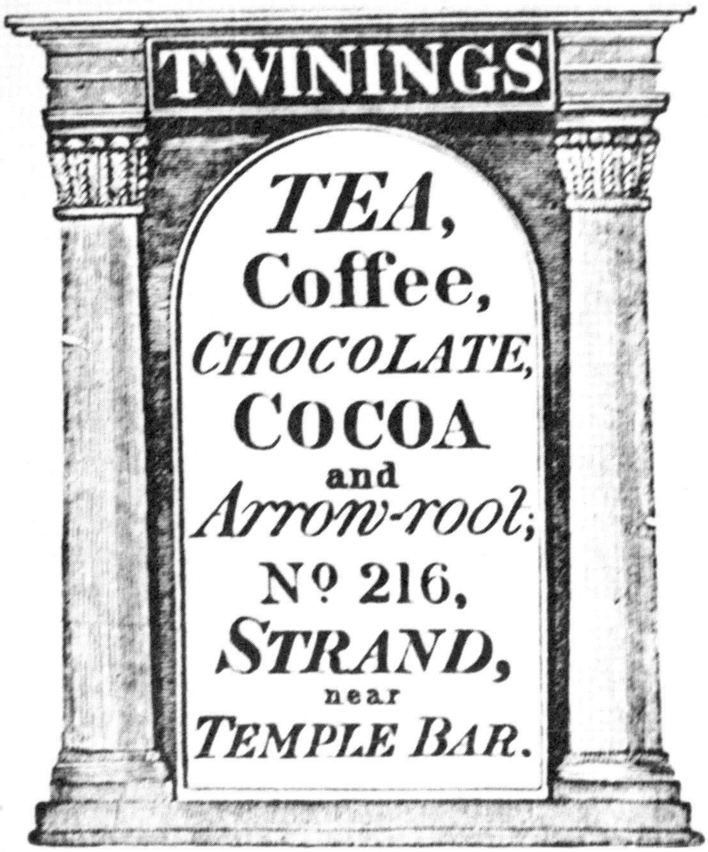


*Two hundred years on, the packaging of Twining's Tea is still designed as it was in the 1780's.*

do, rebuild the city?"

Matter-of-fact Hester found such exchanges embarrassing. That was all in the past, gone long ago and best forgotten.

"No, Jacob, only build a new manufactory behind the three houses. There's room a-plenty. They said years ago – remember? – that Thomas Boulsover's new plate would put us out of business. But silver is still for the discerning. We have orders in hand for two years – and don't forget that Lord Clayburne wants a service now. I need more machines, more metal and more room. Peter and Jonathan are fine smiths, Young Jonathan comes on apace, and we have good workmen. Why can't we do all the work ourselves instead of putting it out?"

"At your time of life? Think first, Hester. Money is not everything, but if you are sure, make a list of what is needed. Remember I lent you the pennies for the drunken parson at the Fleet when you married John? Those pennies were a larger portion of my fortune then than your manufactory could cost me now. You have whatever you require. But I still say you are a mishugge!"

"Thank you, Jacob," said Hester. "We shall draw up the list, Peter and Jonathan and I. The pot, I fear, calls the kettle black!"

The old lady came out into the morning sunshine, retracing her steps along the boundary of the Artillery Ground. Turning into Bunhill Row she paused, observing with satisfaction the well-tended, prosperous aspect of her property. Things had improved since the riots led by Lord George Gordon. Popery was no doubt sinful, but a Protestant zealot at the head of a gin-sodden mob had been no fit instrument to improve the situation. The rioters, thank heaven, had avoided Bunhill Row because they were probably unaware that most of the Volunteers were away guarding the Bank of England. Since that disturbance, much to the satisfaction of the inhabitants, patrols by members of the Artillery Company had made night journeys in the area comparatively safe. The desperadoes and robbers who roamed about and near the City, now found other parishes less hazardous and more rewarding. The odd hungry cur still ventured timorously scavenging to the back doors of the houses, but "Thieving Lane", as it was once called, was becoming almost a respectable thoroughfare, at least at its lower end.

The Parish Register listed several residents of note. Officers and servants of the Artillery Company occupied the houses on the right, where once the King's Archers had stood to their marks with the butts rising clear, far to the north. Then came the tall, narrow dwelling of Jacob Prothero, while Sir James Esdaile's mansion and the Bateman establishment graced the left hand side. Samuel Whitbread, the brewer, occupied a house nearby when he was in London. Up to the top of the Artillery Ground, where stood the mellow, solid piles of Armoury House and St Luke's Vicarage, a satisfying order prevailed, and if vast heaps of rubbish did tend to accumulate beyond the burial ground, at least the situation was no worse than in most other communities on the outskirts of a teeming city. There were green fields and open country within easy walking distance, and thither, when time and money – for the cost of living rose from day to day – permitted, repaired the people of Bunhill Row and the rest of London for leisure if the weather was fine.

Hester walked into the large, ramshackle shed of a building which served as a workshop behind number 107. She was wearing an apron, not the dainty starched and pleated affair which she affected about the house, but the heavy canvas garment of the workman.

Her old work-bench was kept tidy as of right, although for many months now she had not been near it. Its maintenance was the traditional task of the youngest apprentice. He had often wondered why the chore was necessary at all and equated it in his mind with going to church on Sunday. John Bateman had founded the Firm and God had made the world. That must have something to do with it. He paused now, petrified, in the middle of scooping up a little pile of silver lemel and sweepings. Had he forgotten anything? A pair of large, cheeky Cockney eyes looked on apprehensively, but all appeared in order. The bench surface was clear, and John Bateman's tool rack contained its full complement. Nothing had been borrowed.

Hester extracted a small hammer, hefted it gently and put it down. Then she began to study Lady Clayburne's drawing.

Her son Peter laid down the beginnings of a chalice and came over, a worried look on his face. "Mother, what ails you? Is there something we've forgotten? At your time of life you should let us do the work. What is that scribble? Go in the house, Mother. We'll take care of it."

"My time of life, eh?" scoffed Hester. "I may have years, son, but wait for my dotage before you tell me to go home. You think I can't do it? Humour an old woman, Peter. Let me try my skill again. I'll wager I can still fashion a better pot than any of you!"

Hester cut a piece of silver as she spoke, put it through the roller, and then, with the quiet confidence born of long practice, set about the laborious task of hand raising. Peter, observing the curious glances of the workmen, returned to his bench shaking his head. The chorus of chatter, temporarily muted, resumed, and as the old lady struck her shapeless cylinder into plastic form, the workshop vibrated once more into life. As she tapped and moulded, pressed, formed and polished, the rest of the workers caught the rhythm and more was produced that day than at any time during the past six months, Hester Bateman was still a master craftswoman.

In the evening, with a tired soreness of limb, almost but not quite countered by a sense of well-being following a highly rewarding day – even the new apprentice had given her a "Good evenin', Ma'am", with a certain awe-filled deference when she laid down her tools – Hester stood in the doorway of number 107 as had long been her habit after work was done.

The people passed on their way home. Samuel Whitbread acknowledged her for the second time that day. Several young gentlemen passed into the Artillery Ground to take up the evening pickets, for practice on the modern, shortened archery butts, or merely to be sociable over a pot of ale. Significant events in Bunhill Row, even births and deaths, were centred mainly on the Artillery Company, although occasionally an important local personage inconveniently joined John Bunyan in the churchyard. The Honourable Artillery Company gave the place social colour. The inhabitants felt as if they lived in a Royal back garden.

The gentlemen, parading in their uniforms, provided an endless source of gossip. In June there had been a notable casualty, when Major Sir Barnard Turner fell off his horse. The Major's inglorious demise provided excuse for a very satisfying corporate expression of public grief. The Volunteers all sent detachments to escort their colleague on his last journey, which was just as well, since on the way the bailiffs tried to apprehend the corpse for debt! Such episodes consolidated public feeling, made them think of themselves as one big happy family.

In July, on the Artillery Ground, a Mr Edmund Whatmore demonstrated an invention to scale walls in sieges or save lives in case of fire. Hester studied this with interest, reflecting, with her own personal experience in the uses of metal, that a little less preference for timber in the construction of such machines might well make them safer where tinder-dry wood was the material so commonly used for building. The possibility of a conflagration at number 107 was a prime reason to hasten her own rebuilding project, but bricks and mortar were costly.

Now it was August, and, thought Hester, with a slight resurgence of feminine temperament for which she knew she was too old, but which it amused her nevertheless to indulge, it's time for something else to happen.

As if in answer to her whim, a flamboyant, dark-haired lady flounced down the street. Whatever one thought about her, admitted Hester reluctantly as she saw her coming, you had to give her credit for making an impression.

A gown of red velvet trimmed with white lace set off the dark hair and white skin. Widow Walton, no longer young, was still a beauty to stop a man in his tracks and still did.

She had arrived in Bunhill Row some ten years since and occupied a cottage at its upper extremity. A small legacy from an elderly Soho employer had brought her minimal independence. She immediately became the subject of much controversial banter, some of it scandalous.

She was popular with the Artillery officers and, most important, she kept house – that is, she attended daily – to the domestic affairs of Jacob Prothero. She had nothing to do with the Sign of the Sea Horse, but she looked after the small establishment at the corner of Bunhill Row. This provided a comfortable supplement to her income and a much envied freedom. Hester pointedly ignored any ribald conjecture. Molly and she became good friends. What did it matter? What, after all, had two lonely people to lose by offering each other consolation? If Molly Walton was on her way to spend an hour or two with Jacob, then good fortune to them both.

Molly was in a discursive humour.

"Bid you good evening, Mistress Bateman", she said, dabbing with a tiny kerchief and fluttering the draperies. "I trust you prosper."

"Yes, Molly," said Hester. "I find life very pleasant. Wait and I'll fetch us a seat." She brought a pair of small milking stools and the two women arranged themselves in the evening sunshine. All up and down the street those with leisure were doing the same. A laundry maid, having laboured since dawn, passed tiredly up the Row toting a huge laden basket. Two young men smiled as they went toward the Artillery Ground.

Hester waited. Molly was unpredictable, full of enthusiasms. Best let her speak.

"I am all of a flutter, Mistress", she said at length. "I met today the most be-autiful young man – such appearance, Ma'am, such a courageous bearing; such fortitude in adversity. It really is too mortifying that he cannot proceed with his venture. I was about to call upon Sir Watkin to gain his assistance. The poor man was so distracted, Ma'am. It was pitiful".

Occupied with her own schemes Hester had been out of touch with local gossip for several days. Quite what the Captain General of the Honourable Artillery Company could do to assist the ambitions of a beautiful young man she was at a loss to understand. "A distressing situation", was the only comment she could muster. Where did the heart-rending tragedy occur?"

"It's at the Lyceum, Ma'am", continued Molly. "It's the balloon on display there so that those with sufficient appreciation of such a philosophical wonder may subscribe to its advancement". Molly paused in amazement as her own eloquence. "I have a ticket, Ma'am, and I have been to see it three times. It is magnificent! So beautiful; and Lunardi – they call him Vincent, he comes from Naples – oh, my heart bleeds for him!"

The frivolous thought occurred to Hester that if Jacob wished to advance himself in Molly's favour he should immediately buy himself a balloon. She banished it as unworthy.

There was much current talk about balloons. In France and elsewhere, so they said, weights, animals and even people had been carried aloft by smoke confined in a large man-made bubble. Smoke required a fire and fire was dangerous, something you do not treat lightly. But more recently there had been many experiments with vapours. Hester's craft involved the reaction of acids with metals. Some of these were distinctive. What if the vapours could be captured and were lighter than the atmosphere? She had heard of Vincent Lunardi. His plan was based upon some such reasoning.

"Is this . . . beautiful . . . balloon destroyed then, Molly?"

"No, no, Mistress Bateman. Worse than that. His experiment was to be at the Chelsea Hospital, but another creature, seeking to forestall Vincent with another balloon", with feminine unreason, "not half so pretty, was so inept in handling matters that the crowd ran riot! And now poor Vincent is not to be allowed . . . oh, crowds are so vicious, so cruel!"

"Wait", said Hester, understanding at last. "You were not proposing that your Neapolitan should come here! Molly! Consider those multitudes. Do you want them to destroy us?"

Molly did not reply. She was staring across the road at the main entrance to the Artillery Ground. Hester followed her glance in time to catch the sentry offering a salute. Colonel Sir Watkin Lewes, in full regimentals, walked through the gate, accompanied by an elegant beruffled figure gesticulating as he earnestly spoke. Hester had to concede his dark, elegant good looks.

"It's Vincent!" cried Molly, springing up. "He has followed my advice. I am certain Sir Watkin will assist him!"

Hester hoped not, not if a riot were to be the outcome. But this was an era of invention and perhaps she could yet live to see history made. After her eventful day, since Molly had hurried away after Sir Watkin and the hopeful aeronaut, she picked up the stools and retired for an evening repast with the family.

Whether Molly Walton's plea to Sir Watkin was couched in irresistable personal terms, – and he had a reputation with the ladies, – or whether Lunardi's offer of one hundred guineas – he having the support of the Neapolitan Ambassador – for the family of Sir Barnard Turner swung the balance, it will never be known. The Captain General had already refused application from two other balloonists to demonstrate their ability earlier in the year.

Certainly by one means or another Sir Watkin was persuaded in

*Lunardi flies over the artillery ground.*

Lunardi's favour. The new applicant's case to the Court of Assistants was presented to such good effect that a fly-bill, one of many to circulate throughout London, appeared on the main Artillery Ground Gate shortly afterwards. "Mr Vincent Lunardi, Secretary to the Neopolitan Ambassador, will become the First Traveller in the English Atmosphere on the 15th September, 1784."

A bond of £500 against possible damage was required, and the Company would appear under arms to protect the thirty-two-and-a-half foot striped fabric monster from the expected concourse. Bunhill Row awaited the event with considerable interest, to which was added a spice of apprehension, for an optimist by the name of Tyler, and a Frenchman, had barely escaped with their lives after failing to get off the ground in their separate balloons elsewhere.

News of progress in the Lunardi venture was bandied about the Artillery Ground as preparations went forward. Peter Bateman cursed the distraction among his workmen. He also maintained a running protest at his mother's return to her work-bench. But Hester was wise. Her work went steadily forward, interspersed with knitting and tatting and other domestic chores. She did nothing to undermine her son's authority. The workers admired her skill, even competed. Challenge brought interest. There was a new light in the old lady's eye as the service for Lord Clayburne took shape.

Nearly a month, as she had forecast, had passed before it was ready for polishing. The finials on pot and box were a problem. The slight alteration in the basic Bateman proportions completely changed the balance of the finished pieces, and Hester had to cast and re-cast entirely new forms to create an outline to her satisfaction. Now the service was almost ready and Lord Clayburne was calling at the end of the week. He had written to say that he would be walking up from the bank with Jacob Prothero with whom he had business on Friday.

Suddenly the customary even, clattering hum of a metal craftsman's shop was shattered by the youngest apprentice. Returning from an errand, he completely forgot the august presence of the owner of the Firm at her bench. "It's come! That balloon 'as! The soldiers 'ad ter take it out o' the Lyceum 'cos they wanted more money, but it's 'ere! Come in three big carts. Cummanaver look!"

Hester, suppressing a smile, pretended not to hear. The apprentice, suddenly coming to his senses, tried to look as if he was no longer there. Everyone else went on working.

Later, with an almost childish eagerness, Hester came out herself to observe the proceedings. The ascent was not to be until the following day, but already there was activity in the Artillery Ground. An "Engine to Generate the Flammable Gas" was in process of assembly, and the worthy doctor who had invented it, one Fordyce, with a glazed look and unsteady gait indicating a distinct predilection for the bottle, was issuing incomprehensible instructions to his minions. The confusion boded ill for Lunardi's venture. Nevertheless Hester regarded the equipment with interest. She would have questioned the doctor, had he not appeared so distracted, and in any case the already milling crowd would have made intelligent discourse impossible.

Her belief in the interaction of acid and metal to produce vapour, she found, was justified. Here were two cisterns, which must contain acid – she wondered if it was the same aqua fortis they used to test silver – from which a pipe was directed into two large barrels of metal filings, iron, she thought, or zinc. One was enclosed, and from this a long length of silken tube led away to the box-like assemblage, lightly constructed, which was to carry the intrepid astronauts. It was known now that Vincent Lunardi, adopted as a local hero and already a conqueror of maidenly hearts in Bunhill Row, was to be accompanied in his assault upon the atmosphere by his friend, Mr Charles Biggin. The ladies of the area eagerly awaited the arrival of yet another focus for adoration.

The activity continued far into the night. "A shilling says she'll never get off the ground."

"Wager a guinea it blows up. Invention of the devil! Strutting' Macheroni! How d'ye expect a feller like that to do the thing properly? Wait 'til an Englishman builds a balloon!"

"If he do get up in the sky, how's he goin' ter get dahn agin? Like to be blown over the sea or hit St Paul's. Probable 'e's a French spy. Hope 'e gets drownded, comin' 'ere wiv 'is airs an' 'is graces!"

Lunardi, Sir Watkin and several officers were to be seen wandering among the equipment. As the hour advanced, the aeronaut appeared increasingly aggravated by the apparent unconcern of Dr Fordyce, whose efforts so far had done little to fill the huge coloured envelope which lay limply spread upon the grass. Only as it became dark did it look as if the much-vaunted "flammable vapour" was entering the balloon at all, and even then no more than an apparent cushioned arc some three feet high showed evidence of all the activity. An urchin with a stick ran up, tried to poke the growing monster, and was immediately chased off by a harassed and swearing Artilleryman. The urchin thumbed his nose.

All the while the crowds were gathering, right round the Artillery Ground, in the Row, in the graveyard, in Chiswell Street and in Moor Fields on the opposite side. Hester retired late with a sense of foreboding. She had seen Lunardi throw up his hands in despair before disappearing into Armoury House.

The following morning the crowd was so dense that only those living in the immediate neighbourhood arrived for work at the manufactory.

The balloon had at last begun to achieve a semblance of its intended spheroid entity, but when Lunardi came out to look at it his display of Latin temperament was evidence of Fordyce's inadequacy. The Doctor was now obviously drunk, far more concerned with the frightened processes of a flock of sheep lodged in the Artillery Ground overnight by a shepherd who, knowing nothing of the great events going forward, was on his way to market, then the balloon. The antics of an ancient ram seemed to interest him particularly.

In the middle of the turmoil, throwing the military, who were completely

*Vincent Lunardi Esq.*

unprepared, into a frenzy of unrehearsed, well-intended but inept compliments, the Prince of Wales arrived with an equerry, and with enthusiastic bonhomie commenced to question the already distracted launching crew.

Hester watched with her family from a front room window on the third floor above the manufactory. The children would mark the day into their old age. The crowd surged in panic as the cry rose that a bull had got loose from a butcher's pound. An uncertain ensuing calm quickly stirred into renewed, violent agitation as a scaffolding loaded with spectators collapsed. A pick-pocket was taken red-handed and frog-marched, terrified, up the road, for a ducking in the cess pool. Thus, full of alarums and excursions, the morning wore on. The cries, the turmoil of shouted conversation, the deep throating, sweaty respiration of ten thousand people merged into an apprehensive, vibrant afternoon.

As the time for the demonstration approached it appeared that some progress was at last being achieved with the inflation of the balloon. Fortunately a French chemist, Aimè Argand, come to witness the performance, had realised that all was not well and offered assistance. He took over the gas generator from a now gently snoring Dr Fordyce, and although he could not work miracles, the great envelope gradually rose higher.

One o'clock arrived. Half past came and went, then two could be heard chiming out across the City. The vast concourse surged and bubbled like a great cauldron coming to the boil. A pedlar of favours had his display tipped over by a gang of hooligans. Small parties of other ruffians sought destructive diversion. The mood of the crowd was becoming ugly.

Now the military were beginning to realise that in the event of trouble they could do little to hold back the multitude without resorting to arms, a decision not to be taken lightly. Not only public order, but the safety of the Prince, not to mention several M.P.s and notables was at stake. Sir Watkin was seen to approach Lunardi.

A quick decision was vital. The Neapolitan was no coward. To save the situation, with an entirely admirable disregard for his personal safety, he decided to go up with the half-inflated balloon, alone.

He placed in the basket a dog, whose terrified barking was taken by the multitude as enthusiastic approval of the venture, a cat in a tied wicker basket, which strenuously and noisily resented her canine companion, and a pigeon in an open-sided and netted box. The bird regarded the whole proceedings with pert disdain, probably having been a permanent resident of the Artillery Ground and on his home-beat, so to speak. A bottle of wine and a cold roast chicken became confused with the ballast.

Now that he was irrevocably committed to the adventure, Lunardi's mood changed from harassed, hysterical gloom to devil-may-care optimism. Squaring his shoulders he crossed himself, which caused some cat-calls and general hostility from those protestants standing nearest. Then he bowed to the assembled company. The crowd responded with some applause and a few ironic cheers which were picked up and repeated into the distance in waves. It was obvious that many there refused to believe that the huge, multi-coloured bag could leave terra-firma. But Lunardi looked steadily at the heavens, his lips moving.

*John Bunyan's tomb, St. Luke's Churchyard, Bunhill Row, London E.C.2.*

Then, amid renewed shouts, and to more cries of protest from his unlikely fellow-passengers,he stepped into the basket, paused yet again, and picked up his megaphone.

"Cast away!" The command took the numerous helpers and hangers-on by surprise, but the sudden roar of the crowd provoked an excited untying and releasing of every rope in sight. One helper, tardy in letting go, was almost taken into the air, thereby nearly upsetting the basket and the whole enterprise. The dog and the cat were both hysterical.

Lunardi now commenced to jettison his ballast like an emperor distributing largesse, and slowly, almost reluctantly, as the crowd scrambled for souvenirs, the great red and blue monster took to the air, carrying, with rising impetus, the intrepid aeronaut up and over the craning, cheering concourse.

The Prince, convinced that the foolhardy balloonist would never again return to earth, doffed his hat in silent tribute, and those about him, always quick to ape the mannerisms of their fashionable leader, did likewise. "Wouldn't fancy the Macheroni's chances," said he, and someone, with a mistakenly pious intonation, uttered "Amen."

The crowd still cheered wildly. As the balloon rose, Lunardi could be seen toasting the spectators with his bottle. Before sailing away above the trees to the north, where one of the oars, which he appeared to have produced from nowhere to aid his progress, suddenly broke and fell with little apparent deterrent effect, he had thrown out both the bottle, and a letter secured with a napkin to his corkscrew. The crowd, with necks craned, watched the gay sphere with its swinging basket until it became a tiny spot and vanished. Some went home. Others stayed to make holiday far into the night. Peter Bateman shepherded his workmen back to their benches.

Next day, a traveller arriving on the Manchester Post brought news that Lunardi had come down safely in a field at Ware in Hertfordshire, only the cat having suffered from the cold, high atmosphere. The H.A.C. honoured him. They made him an honorary Member, and it amused him thereafter to tell his admirers in his slightly accented English that he was an honorary Member of the Honourable Artillery Company. Cosway painted him.

Hester's sense of foreboding was not dispelled. She worked late to finish the Clayburne service. She wanted her last major production to be perfect. His Lordship was due on the morrow.

Jacob Prothero had watched the ascent from the back window of his house. Widow Walton was with him. She prepared a meal in the evening and lingered late until the crowds had melted somewhat. As it was growing dark and the evening was fine, she accepted his offer to escort her to the top of Bunhill Row.

Outside her little house, one of very few which sported a garden, Jacob, with unaccustomed tenderness, took Molly's hand and raised it to his lips. The day had been full of other peoples' excitement. The sight of family groups out for the day, of young men on the threshold of life's adventure, even of the foolhardy but romantic Lunardi himself made the banker feel lonely. What was a fortune worth when time was running out? "Good-night, Molly," he said, smiling, it seemed, reminiscently. "Thank you for a very good day."

There was no need for hurry. The moon shone high and the reminiscent mood persisted. The artillery picket passed along the road, voices raised in jocular abandon as they greeted him. They had fortified their spirits against the night with deep draughts of Whitbread's best brew. Their mere presence brought assurance against the shadows.

Jacob turned into the burial ground and stood by the pile that marked the resting place of John Bunyan. A dapple of moonlight shone across the heaving sward. This, he thought, was a strange, a loveable country, a refuge for the homeless wanderer. Where else in the world was such security to be found? And yet England, to some, appeared to reel under the constant hammering of a malignant fate. She had lost her American Colonies, squandered her assets on several wars, suffered internal unrest. In spite of all this, she bred greatness; the creator of Pilgrim's Progress, Shakespeare, Wren, even characters like his friend, Hester Bateman. He sighed and shook his head, passing from moonlight under the trees.

The two ill-clad, lean and hungry shadows had followed silently, close behind the Artillery Patrol, judging shrewdly that where they had passed lay safety.

Jacob felt nothing. The blow from the loaded blackjack was mercifully swift, and it crushed his skull. The marauders got nothing but a velvet coat with silver buttons and a little loose change, for Jacob Prothero, provident as ever, had left his gold watch with the jewelled fob, his wallet, even his seal, in his chamber in Bunhill Row. The buttons bore Hester Bateman's mark and one of the robbers was taken when he tried to sell Jacob's coat on the following day.

In his will, against which Jacob's son Israel protested at length, Molly Walton was left £500, and was thereafter considered a wealthy woman.

And Hester?

In a long full life this wasn't the first time she had encountered death. With a passionate belief in a better world to come, she was more concerned with the living. Like Jacob she believed that there should always be someone to "take care of the shop". When John died, since he had paid her the ultimate compliment of leaving her his tools, she had had his will proved within hours of his death and proceeded forthwith to found a small dynasty. No disrespect; mourning served no useful purpose.

Israel Prothero took over the bank at the sign of the Sea Horse. He was not a young man and for many years he had considered that his father was too careful. His ambitions to modernise had been fettered for too long. The bank must be rebuilt. Tuttle and his contemporaries should be retired. The world was full of opportunities if one was ruthless enough.

Hester Bateman took her business elsewhere when Molly's legacy was questioned, and Israel withdrew his objections in an effort to save the situation. Israel nearly lost the Clayburne account too, and only the intricacies of the many investments, the ramifications of properties and trusts with which the bank had dealt for so many years, made a transfer unthinkable.

Hester watched her sons take up a new challenge. They worked even harder. In two years they were able to finance their own expansion.

# Squire's Teapot

The Paxham Orphanage Governors sat self-righteously in session. The Beadle, Mr Pennyfeather, sweating in his official buttoned blue serge, breathlessly reported the progress of affairs in the year 1797. The day was warm. Parson Porter suffered a vague qualm of sympathy for his weekly congregation as his eyelids grew heavy. A dusty ray of sunshine shafted through the window and a weaving concourse of house-flies busied itself over the long table to the general distraction.

Mrs Pennyfeather was in charge of the place.

The fourteen inmates, young varmints all, said the Beadle, with an eye on His Lordship, whose attention, at the head of the table, was inclined to waver, were her pride and joy.

"But fourteen's quite a few, an' they cost money. An' how long can our gen'rous – oh, so gen'rous – benefactors, be expected to dip into their pockits? Bad to the core they are, lazy too, wuss the older they gets. One in partic'lar won't do wat 'e's told. Bin 'ere too long."

The pottery spitoon by his right foot occupied his wheezy attention for a long moment.

"You'd think after all Mrs P's kindness there'd be some gratitood – after all 'er slavin' – treats 'em like 'er own she do; but that one's past it I reckon.

"The little 'uns is diff'rent. You can make 'em obedjent. Just 'aveter show 'em the birch an' they're good as gold. But once they gets ter nine or ten they should be out workin' fer their keep. The labourer" – this, unexpectedly, directed at the dozing parson – "should earn his hire!"

Mr Pennyfeather, gratified by the startled glance with which the dozing cleric returned to consciousness, puffed out his cheeks and tried to look impressive.

" 'E oughter be put ter work. Upsets the uvvers with 'is ideas. Young Fibb 'is name is, William Fibb. Wants ter go fer a soldier. Sent 'im down to Mister Morley las' week fer a mute at old Dame Crackett's fun'ral an' wot 'appens? 'E 'as ter set up whistlin' British Grenadiers as they're puttin' down the coffin."

"Yes, indeed, indeed, hum," agreed Mr Morley, the wheelwright and undertaker, sitting solemnly in his greening black, eyeing the company with a calculating eye. He could size up a body to the inch and compensated for his unctuous inferiority by working out, privately of course, the value as corpses of any gathering in which he felt uncomfortable. "Churchyard's no place to show one's loyalty in."

The subject of Mr and Mrs Beadle's displeasure was incarcerated in a tiny locked closet known to Paxham orphans as The Black 'Ole.

No-one, least of all an independent spirit like William, would have chosen to be cast upon village charity. He remembered his father as a red-coated, tobacco smoking giant upon whose massive hallooing shoulders he had been galloped round the village green. He remembered him playing a tin whistle, making a kite and telling tales of big battles with the Frenchies. His mother he recalled only as someone soft and quietly spoken who kept the tiny cottage neat and shining.

One day she was no longer there, and William, without fully comprehending, found himself sleeping in a bunk in an orphanage which stank of gin, instead of on his own sweet-smelling mattress at home.

Mrs Pennyfeather, like her husband, was large and black, her extremities somewhat frayed and greasy. She wore big hats with feathers in them on very hot days. Her taste for the juniper not only tainted the orphanage; it also made her moods uncertain. One never knew when the large wooden spoon for serving the meagre portions of skilly and slops from the two iron pots in the kitchen would double as a weapon. A lump of greasy gristle on your wooden platter or a clump on the head with a wooden spoon were hazards of life. Either way, they were better than bread and water in the Black 'Ole.

For the past week, Mrs Pennyfeather had waged a one-sided battle with William.

It started on the Monday when he and six diminutive helpers had been set to sweep the yard. William saw no reason why a tedious chore should not be given a little added interest, and livened the exercise with a military flavour. He contrived a series of drills and manoeuvres with the shovels and besoms. Mrs Pennyfeather interrupted an original variation of porting muskets, called William an ungrateful perisher and condemned him to bread and water for the day. Nothing went right thereafter. A simple errand to the village shop produced a brush with a stable lad from the Hall, who laughed at William's simulation of a ceremonial military step along the cobbles by the forge.

William's black eye was of less concern to Mrs Pennyfeather than the jug he left in fragments in a ditch, and by Wednesday he was exceedingly hungry. On Thursday, he kept out of trouble long enough to be fed. On Friday a parcel carried to an outlying farm earned him a bonus of beef and dumplings from a sympathetic farmer's wife, thus proving to his own satisfaction at least, the Beadle's interesting, if confused logic. "Too much vittals," he would say, balancing himself solidly against his own adipos tissue, "finds devil's work for idle fingers."

In the face of such profundity Mrs Pennyfeather was wont to nod solemnly and take another sip of gin.

"Quite right, Mr P. I agree entirely with them sentiments. Needs to be found employment, that one, double quick, afore the 'ole establishment is burned down about our 'eads." A very fat hand moved, it seemed independently, to take up a glass that wasn't there.

"They could do . . . ah . . . with a hand up at Crackett's Farm," said Mr Morley, "but in view of the funeral I don't – ah – hm – believe . . ."

"Come now, Morley." Lord Clayburne was anxious to bring the meeting to some kind of conclusion. "We make too much, surely, of a childish prank. Crackett's not an unreasonable man. A little strict, perhaps, but a little discipline never harmed a lively lad. This one just seems to have plenty of spirit. Knew his father well. Good, honest stock. Shouldn't be any bad blood there. I'll have a word with Crackett."

Thus providentially was the future of William Fibb, of Paxham in Kent, whose forebears were noted in the old, musty Church Register from the sixteenth century, set upon its course. A lesser character might have meekly accepted his fate. Not so William; he still had a score to settle.

The climax of an orphanage week, disregarding holidays, was the weekly parade to the church of St Peter on the green. Parson Porter was a strong believer in the deterrent influence of Hell, and each week he pulverised the village with a harangue upon its wickednesses, comparing its denizens unfavourably with those of Sodon and Gomorrah. He continued to rant and rave with persistent fervour for exactly half-an-hour by the sand in his pulpit glass. That was enough.

Paxham Village enjoyed its church. It was the focus of village life. All the Paxhamites turned out in Sunday finery, listened with corporate, open-mouthed masochism to the parson, lustily supported the temperamental old organ in three rousing hymns and wallowed afterwards in an orgy of gossip among the lichened gravestones. They strayed in companionable groups under the old oak tree on the edge of the green which had sheltered Paxham courtships for centuries.

The building was sited very close to an ageless pilgrim track dating, so 'twas said, from the twelfth century.

The Clayburnes, from the evidence, had been in Paxham a very long time. An incised, hooded and mailed Sir Vincent reclined, his crossed legs resting upon an indeterminate beast resembling a passant poodle, upon a well-worn brass in the aisle. His demise was marked in the year thirteen-hundred-and-ninety-two. In the seventeenth century two other Clayburnes were commemorated in more solid form. Sir Grantley Clayburne, Kt., and his lady, lay side by side on a catafalque at the back of the church beside the font., he elaborately clad in half armour, she elegantly robed. Strange dress, thought William, for going to bed.

William, who fortunately enjoyed a tough constitution, also had a lively imagination. Each Sunday, usually standing – for only the best-behaved orphans were allowed to grace the back pew with their presence – he regarded the prostrate figures with a feeling which wavered between anticipation and apprehension. They appeared to be sleeping peacefully, but Parson Porter had been a little strong on the Last Trump for several weeks, bellowing loudly enough to wake the soundest sleeper. What if the petrified couple suddenly sat up during the sermon? How would the valiant knight fare in his stony armour suiting?

On that momentous Sunday, with the imminent termination of his orphanage sojourn uppermost, in his thoughts, William could hardly contain himself. He shuffled from one bare foot to the other, scratched his unwashed pate and rattled the marbles in the pocket of his smock, drawing from Mrs Pennyfeather an eloquent glare of irate righteousness, which, since it had to be withdrawn from the pulpit, acted like a prop removed from a scaffold. It didn't tumble the edifice, but it caused it to falter momentarily. The parson, sensing a rival focus, stared back, lost his place, and closed the sermon abruptly. Then came the great consummation. Mrs Pennyfeather scratched the back of her neck; she scratched again, grew very red in the face and appeared to suffer from a violent internal disturbance.

Over William's face there spread a seraphic grin as he stood, stock still now, to await developments.

During the week, smarting under the constant weight of insult and thoughtless repression, William had retired to shed a few resentful tears in a corner of the room where most of the orphanage communal activities took place. A long deal table and a pair of matching forms, scrubbed into splinters, a great old oaken cupboard and a grandfather clock with a single hand set at three o'clock, these and the bunk beds were almost the only concessions to the charitable objectives of the establishment. On the floor behind the cupboard – the corner was cleaner than usual having been swept and swept again in honour of the Governors' visit – William had sat brooding upon the unfairness of life generally. Under a break in the plaster and stone, revealed by the repeated sweeping, was an ants' nest. And the ants, with their refuge disturbed, spilled and seethed among the dust.

On Saturday night, while the Beadle and his wife were commiserating over a bottle, upon the combined ingratitude of the Orphanage inmates, a colony of ants suffered an enforced migration. From queen to newest larvae, they were scooped into a grimy kerchief and released beneath an untidy welter of limp linen, in the top drawer of Mrs Pennyfeather's chest of drawers.

William, hugging his secret to his scrawny chest, walked on air as fourteen hungry orphans, under the distracted supervision of Mrs Pennyfeather, returned with unaccustomed haste, to find refuge for a monumental scratch. Her charges followed blithely enough. For once their high spirits remained unreprimanded. And even yet another helping of watery stew was better than no food at all – if you were allowed to enjoy it.

Not many events in Paxham Orphanage were worthy of celebration, not, at any rate by the inmates. There were, of course the high points of the conker season, when the dispute as to whether a single victory by a virgin conker, however baked or treated in the sun, over a seasoned "hundreder", automatically made the newcomer into a "hundred-and-oner", annually burgeoned as it does today. The owner no doubt enjoyed his triumph with his friends of the moment. So did the possessor of a particularly successful Glarney when marbles were in season.

But here, since William had circulated news of his adventure with the ants, was a coup to be enjoyed by all.

Fourteen orphans had lain that night in their austere and comfortless bunks in an expectant ecstasy and an orgy of fidgets which would have betrayed their anticipation to anyone only slightly more sensitive than the Pennyfeathers.

First Mrs Pennyfeather was heard to mount the stairs, to be followed very shortly by a heavily breathing Beadle. Did Mrs P. sleep in one of her hats? None knew, since she had never been seen without. There came then a short interlude of conversation, a clatter of disgarded footwear, and a protesting wheeze from the strapping of the affronted four-poster as two heavy bodies rested on it. Then followed a silence.

But only for a very short while. From the sudden activity, the scurrying, cursing, and general disturbance, it was obvious that William had chosen his point of attack well. The vast defences of Mrs Pennyfeather's night attire had been breached!

A memorable night for the orphans of Paxham.

A memorable night, followed by a significant morning. Very early, before he had even broken his fast, William was seized by an ear and led by the Beadle, at distasteful arm's length, up to Crackett's Farm.

His resistance to authority had become almost instinctive, and he did not immediately realise that his situation had improved. True, he was now regularly fed, not with watery stew and scraps, but with wholesome dishes from Dame Crackett's kitchen. But that formidable, if kindly lady also scrubbed him down from head to foot in a large tub at least once a week and he was constantly reminded that there was running water to be had a-plenty from the pump in the yard. But life was better than it had been. Mrs Crackett made him clothes. And once the sullen reaction to adult advances, the result of many years of Pennyfeather repression, had been softened by kindness, she introduced her protege to the old horn book which had been gathering dust in a dresser drawer since her girlhood. She had no children of her own.

The chores about a farm are never light. William had to work hard for his keep. Milking, mucking out, grooming, feeding cattle, pigs or chickens, hoeing, mowing, ploughing, sowing, reaping, threshing, thatching, stacking, were only part of the daily round. Before the sun was up William was abroad, fetching and carrying, sweeping, polishing and scraping. Farmer Crackett himself worked hard, and while he laboured he saw no reason for idleness in others. Thus William had little opportunity to indulge the whims and fancies of childhood. He made imaginary military dispositions with the animals and attempted to drill the chickens with disastrous effects upon their laying capacity. Not often was he permitted to sit in the big, warm kitchen beneath the framed print of the Eye of God which dominated the wall opposite the massive iron range. Only infrequently did he benefit from Mrs Crackett's instruction, but he had a capacity for learning. The horn book carried the key to letters and with that and the huge family bible, to which he was permitted access when his aptitude was discovered, he soon began to read.

Summer came and went, a cycle of plough and harvest, a sequence of marbles, peg-tops and conkers although for these he had little leisure. He added several inches to his stature, was less cowed, and was soon no more likely to be involved in mischief than any other lusty youngster of ten years, but nothing could daunt his military ambitions.

One morning as he pulled turnips, a strange sound drifted up from the village. A heavy iron-shod dray had just passed clamorously up the stony track on the other side of the hedge, and as the clip-clop of the horses faded away, the beat was taken up in a stirring rhythm, backed almost

*A recruiting party on the Portsmouth Road in 1769 from the original by J. Collett.*

immediately by a reedy but compelling melody. The sound of fife and drum beckoned. Without a thought William cast down his last turnip and ran helter skelter down to the green, just in time to witness the arrival of a group which took his young, gaping attention to the exclusion of all else.

A recruiting Serjeant from the Royal Artillery, flanked on one side by a boy soldier with a big drum, and a diminutive fifer on the other, had already enlisted several likely village lads. He stood beneath the oak tree, haranguing a mixed company with a stirring summons to the colours, a well-rehearsed call to fight for His Majesty. William was completely carried away by reference to "rattling muskets," "cannons roaring", and "colours flying". At the cry of "Victory, lads!" he presented himself, straight as a ramrod somewhere on a level with the Serjeant's crossbelt. In the rather startled silence which followed this unexpectedly patriotic gesture his piping treble clamoured, "If you please, Sir, would you take I for a sodger?"

The new recruits cheered, the onlookers laughed, and the Serjeant patted William condescendingly on the head.

"I'm as big as that there fifer!"

As he said, it, William put his hand on the big drum, receiving promptly his first lesson in military discipline. The drumhead was sacred. A sharp tap on the knuckles rewarded his presumption; up went his grimy fists as he eyed the robust figure of the drummer, considered the kettle drummers who stood behind the Serjeant and wondered which side the Serjeant or the villagers would support. Then he bethought himself of his father's uniform, and with a latent memory of something he had heard somewhere about a respect for the King's Livery, he turned on his heel without a word and walked slowly back to the turnip field, feet dragging as he thoughtfully scuffed up the summer dust.

William's dream of military glory had received new stimulus from the sight of that diminutive fifer. The call to arms swept through the whole country. The war in America was over, but there were armies still in India and Holland and the West Indies, naval forces too, and now Napoleon was busy in Italy. There was talk, particularly among the young, of the new experimental regiments. William had long since made up his mind to follow in his father's footsteps. He too would go to war. But how to achieve that significant transformation from civilian to military status?

On a bitter December day, when a battery of the Royal Horse Artillery passed near the village bound for their City headquarters, William could no longer resist the call. Making sure that his master and mistress were nowhere in evidence he stifled a slight pang of conscience, helped himself to half a loaf and a large portion of cheese from the larder, and followed the soldiers to their overnight quarters at Blackheath.

Sixteen miles he marched that day, numb with the effort of his diminutive legs to keep step, his nailed high-lows raising blisters on his heels. And, as the tack of drum urged him on, he dreamed of the moment when, confronting the Colonel, he would make his entree into the world military. The great man, a passing soldier told him laughingly, supped at the King's Head.

Cold and hungry, for he dare not fall behind to open his kerchief of rations, William pressed on, to be rewarded at last, in the mist of the early dusk, by sight of the twinkling lights of Blackheath spreading like a misplaced milky way along the depression of Tranquil Vale.

The file wound up past the King's Head and away across the Heath, leaving William now terribly alone and dog-tired, apprehensively eyeing the swinging sign wherefrom the Martyr King stared back with a forbidding squint. He sat, shivering on a mounting block to consider the next move.

An ostler appeared from the coachyard, mopping his brow. A miscellany of leathers hung on his shoulder, and as he walked he gave a desultory

*Tranquil Vale, Blackheath, where young William Fibb would have sought the Colonel in the Kings Head.*

rub to a brass buckle. Then he sat down beside William, who had now transferred his attention from Charles the First. "Cold night to be out, young 'un. Goin' far?"

"P-p-please, Sir, could I get to see the Colonel?"

"Hey, sonny, that's a tall order. Doubt His Nibs upstairs'll be troubling hisself wi' the likes o' you. If it's not too impertinent, like, might one ask what business a young cocksparrer'd be wanting with the gentry? He's at dinner wi' the officers, be busy for hours yet."

William just sat. He didn't know what to say. He opened his mouth but no sound issued forth. He tried again, dashed away the tear which, unbidden, traced a grimy course down his cheek. "I want to go for a sodger, Sir!" Then he just toppled off the stone onto the icy, cobbled ground.

The ostler was a kind-hearted man with sons of his own. One of the kitchen maids was friendly with a gunner who knew one of the Colonel's grooms. The Colonel too had sons of his own and William came to in the best banqueting room on the first floor of the hostelry, as someone poured a fiery liquid down his throat. He coughed, spluttered, and sat up.

He lay on a couch beneath a huge chandelier from which the light of some twenty candles scintillated. They seemed to revolve, to come and go. He shut and opened his eyes again, became conscious of a roisterous company of red and blue, of a hand lifting his head, and a sick-making brandy smell of more of the fiery liquid under his nose.

"Well, my fine young rustic," said the Colonel. "And what may be your pleasure? They say it was me you asked for and you look as if you've come a long way."

"I only want to be a sodger, Sir," said William.

A guffaw from several throats died abruptly as the company discovered that the Colonel was not amused. Meanwhile, William, not understanding the situation, started to join in. The Colonel regarded him gravely.

"I'm ten, Sir, an' I'm big enough for a fifer. I can play a whistle, Sir, and I do have some letters." William stood up unsteadily, pulled at his farmer's smock, regarded his muddy, awkward footwear. He felt shabby against the military finery. "An' Sir . . .," the Colonel placed a hand on his shoulder as he faltered. "I'm cold, Sir, an' I've marched all the way from Paxham —"

The Colonel led William to the table, piled a plate with undreamed delicacies and watched him eat.

Alas for William. The officers all plied him with food. They left coins beside his plate which, later, he tallied to a whole fifteen shillings. He was made to sleep on a settle near the huge, open log-stacked fireplace, but in the morning, when the Colonel re-appeared, it was only to bring the news that soldiering was not yet for him.

"But, young Will," he continued, "it's Paxham ye come from and that, if my memory serves, is Clayburne's place. Went to school with Clayburne. Good feller. Have you . . . ah . . . met His Lordship?"

"Don't think he'd do much, Sir. He was one of the governors of the orphanage, Sir."

"Orphanage, eh?" pondered the Colonel, recalling the irksome responsibilities of his own squireship, cared for now by his less adventurous younger brother. It was not always comfortable to observe the victims of remote charity at close quarters.

In spite of tearful protest, the Colonel's actions were kindly but firm. William was sent, on a saddle horse, this time, and in the company of a Corporal, all the way back to Crackett's Farm. Farmer Crackett took little account of either the Corporal's advice or the transmitted recommendations of the Colonel. "You'll have to return to your master, young Will," he had said. "Can't turn your back on the enemy, what? And be honest, boy, he's given you a roof when you might have had nothing at all. Best face up like a man. I'll write to old Clayburne and see what may be arranged."

So William received what he considered an entirely unmerited thrashing for his "base ingratitude" – indeed Mrs Crackett had searched the entire village for him – and the theft from the larder. The Beadle held forth for a whole hour in 'The Coach and Horses' upon his erstwhile lodger's evil propensities and his certain destination in the future, a dark and violent Bad End. Mr Morley said he'd seen it coming.

Meanwhile, the Corporal proceeded onwards to the Hall, where he delivered a personal letter to Lord Clayburne from his old schoolfriend, Colonel Swinton.

The letter was persuasive. It recalled past times and escapades nearly forgotten. It drew attention to the military ambitions of Master William Fibb, remarked upon his "likely" potentialities and commendable bearing and courage. It suggested that, with suitable sponsorship, he might, when he was twelve, prove acceptable as a recruit into one of the new experimental regiments.

The Colonel, presuming further upon friendship, permitted himself a slight philosophical digression upon the undesirable – nay, even tragic consequence of suppressing such enthusiasm as William's, particularly in an age where the qualities of the rising generation fell so sadly short of the standards to which they had been accustomed when they were young.

"Old hypocrite," muttered His Lordship. "Always in trouble. Never even gave me back that sovereign." But he remained thoughtful. Those poor little devils couldn't have much of a time with the Pennyfeathers. Mr Graves, the Clayburne tutor, was a good fellow, had the right ideas. He had been suggesting more companionship for the Squire's heir for months, said the boy was becoming over-bookish. Difficult to strike a balance when the social round passed you by, and since his wife died life at the Hall had become pretty humdrum. He sought out Mr Graves where he sat, engrossed in the collation of a new acquisition recently arrived from London, an erudite volume in latin, in the library. He showed him the letter.

"What d'ye think, Mr Graves?" said His Lordship. "Have you seen this lad? Seems he walked all the way to Blackheath."

"He'd do Master Richard a power of good," replied the tutor. "I saw young William down watching the recruiting party on the Green. Stepped up large as life. Told them he wanted to be a soldier. Someone rapped his knuckles with a drumstick and he was ready to tackle the whole lot of 'em – you could see it – but he never lost his temper. Crackett was telling me only the other day how highly he thinks of him, too. He thought the march to Blackheath quite a jape. Yes, I'm sure it would be a good thing all round."

The following morning, William, chastened by the ignominy of his return and very sore of person, was fetching potatoes from the clamp. The future seemed bleak enough, but with youthful resilience he drew comfort from a particularly large and ugly tuber, which, he decided, with very little adapting and a pair of peas attached by steel pins for eyes, could be transformed into a likeness of Mrs Pennyfeather. He heard voices, and to his surprise, observed Mrs Crackett leading a file of personages along the hedge from the gate. Behind her came Mr Graves the tutor, whom he had observed in the Clayburne pew on Sunday. Then came the young Viscount Richard whom he hated on sight from the very velvety propriety of his small person. There followed Mr Briggs, the groom, recognisable from afar by his yellow breeches, shining boots and blue and yellow livery weskitt, silver buttons winking in the sun.

To William such a visitation could only mean trouble, but since he could recall no misdemeanour in which he had been involved recently which might have displeased the gentry, and in any case he felt that his own stock having sunk so low it could scarcely fall further, he clasped his potato tightly, stood back against the hedge and awaited developments.

Mrs Crackett and the visitors stopped before him. "That's William," she said baldly. "Will, bid the gentlemen good day. Mr Graves has something to say to you." And then, surprisingly, she turned away and dabbed her eye with her kerchief. William's intended greeting stuck in his throat.

Silence. Viscount Richard was the first to speak. "Good morning, William" he said, and when William said nothing, added "what's that you're holding?"

"It's a spud, a big one."

"Show it to me."

"Shan't!"

The assembled company observed the encounter with astonishment.

"I only want to look at it."

"It's mine!"

Suddenly, as Mrs Crackett screamed and Mr Briggs made indeterminate clucking noises the two flew at each other. Over and over they rolled in the mud and in a very few seconds homespun and velvet, lace and shoddy mingled in a glory of Kentish clay. Only Mr Graves remained unpreturbed. With unerring accuracy he seized two elusive scruffs from the writhing mass and hauled the pair of protesting figures to their feet.

"That's no way to fight, lads," he said. "If you'll just wait until tomorrow I'll show you how to put your fists up properly. Shake hands on it."

Thus, once again, was William's fate set upon a new tangent.

His transformation was not without misgiving. Farmer and Mrs Crackett had provided the only security he had known, and for all their strictures, they had, within their own lights, treated him much as they would a son of their own. Soldiering was William's chosen lot, that he had decided long ago, and he was safe at Crackett's until such time as His Majesty chose to take him. Mr Graves had to produce convincing argument as to the general intention before he agreed to leave for the Hall, and then William only consented to go after Mrs Crackett had spoken in support of Mr Graves and the groom. "They're right, Will," she said. "His Lordship'll look after you better than we can and you're not going far. You can always come up to the farm."

At last William gave in. Mr Briggs took his hand. Mr Graves and Richard followed, away and across the fields to his new home. As he went he hoped they would send on his special things. There was the big bag of marbles, for he had had a successful season, and there were his peg-tops and the lucky but stinking hare's foot which hung in the barn, but you couldn't expect mere grown-ups to grasp the importance of things like that.

The two boys were taken first to the Briggs' cottage to be made fit for presentation to His Lordship. William stood in the drive in wonder, wriggled his muddy toes in the fresh gravel, saw for the first time the greenness of an expanse of tended lawn and then discovered, to his confusion, that he still grasped the potato. He looked at his new friends, solemnly shook hands with Richard, and with a mighty shout flung his burden high over an ornately fashioned yew hedge.

Within an hour the transformation was complete. No velvet – William wouldn't yet sink to that – but suitable attire was found for both the boys, and Mr Graves led the way into Lord Clayburne's library.

The Squire, William discovered, was no wit as terrifying as he had appeared high on his hunter or in his carriage, to an orphanage lad at ground level. Grey-haired and elegant, he offered a hand to the new arrival. "You'll do very well, I believe, providing we keep away from large potatoes! Knew your father. If you want anything, tell Mr Graves. Will you take a dish of tea?"

William was not sure about tea. He watched, fascinated, as a butler brought a silver tray with a teapot, a jug and a bowl upon it. He watched the silver kettle boil over a spirit lamp and saw hot water poured into the pot; then, after the brew had been left to stand, a maid carefully tipped small quantities into tiny bowls which stood in matching dishes of china. Each solemnly raised his cup, using the thumb and forefinger of both hands, sipping the contents slowly. He didn't think much of the tea, but his eye was taken by the pot.

"It's pretty," he said.

"So it is, boy, and interesting too. Made by a remarkable old lady, yes, a lady, in London – Mrs Bateman. See that pattern all round the edge? – it's called beeding. That and the brightcutting are typical of her work."

"Please, Sir, what's typical?"

"It means it's like all the other tea things she made, only this one isn't quite. You see, when I was in London once I went to see Mistress Bateman's manufactory with Mr Prothero – he was the father of my banker – and Lady Clayburne had made a drawing of the tea service she wished to have for her birthday. This is what Mistress Bateman made. 'Tis strange to find a woman with a craft, stranger when she's so skilful at it. Not the thing at all. Woman's place should be in the home, cookin' and sewin', not makin' teapots."

William agreed. He felt comfortably absorbed into masculine society. Although he never really took the fashionable habit of tea drinking, the "typical teapot which wasn't" became a family joke, a symbol of his new life-style.

So William came to Clayburne, and slept once more in a bed with sweet, fresh-smelling linen. At first he found life strange, preferring to work with the grooms in the stables rather than study books in the schoolroom. But Mr Graves and young Richard had taken a liking to the young, rumbustuous son of a soldier. William had a natural appetite for letters, and the library at Clayburne finally tempted him. He commenced to read vastly and took readily to the quill. He learned the things to which a young country gentleman is born, to ride, to shoot, to hunt the otter, badger and fox, to put up his fists and wield a bat with grace. Two years were far too quick in the passing.

Lord Clayburne was good as his word. One summer's morning William Fibb, with young Richard and Mr Graves to see him on his way, waited outside the Coach and Horses for the Post, the carriage which would take him on the first stage of the journey to Colchester, where, at the ripe age of twelve years, he was to be enlisted.

The new recruit had grown. No longer the cowed orphan, he chatted easily with his friends, and if he felt any qualms at leaving them, his manner showed only excitement and a supreme confidence, a willingness to meet a daunting future on its own terms. He felt no end of a dog in his new coat, new hat, new shoes, in short, new everything, and evinced no surprise that even at half-past six in the morning many of those who had only recently forecast his imminent downfall, had now turned out to see him on his way with every evidence of goodwill.

No Beadle came, for by some diverse means the tale of the ants had reached gossiping ears, but the Parson was there, and Mr Morley. Mistress Crackett arrived with an apple-pie and a large piece of cheese done up in a red kerchief, and when, in a flurry of dust, the coach arrived and the horses were being changed, he remarked that the spare vittals presented by his well-wishers would feed all the passengers, both inside and out, for a week.

But, in spite of all his outward display, a lump came to William's throat, as, with a flourish on the horn, a rattle of harness and a great barking of dogs, the coach sped off along the road which would lead, eventually, to London and Charing Cross. He looked back over his shoulder, but already a bend hid his waving friends. He was alone.

By his Lordship's generosity he sat on top, between the coachman and a portly gentleman in a beaver hat and, although the day promised warmth, a variety of capes. This personage addressed the coachman by his christian name of "Jack", a habit indulged, so had said Mr Graves, only by the most seasoned travellers.

William felt in his pocket for the comforting roundnesses of his first allowance, two silver crowns, wondering wistfully if a highwayman might step from a thicket and offer grim choice of money or life. He then realised that the great musket in its basket was so impeded by the chattels of an apple-cheeked matron who rode inside, that the encounter would, perhaps, best be avoided.

As he pondered, the beaver-hatted gentleman enquired his age.

"Fourteen, Sir," he lied. "And I'm going for a soldier."

"That's a fine, patriotic profession, don't you think, Jack?" said the gentleman, with a huge wink. "Make a good soldier, you will."

They passed, as the conversation, or more truly the monologue, of the beaver-hatted gentleman progressed, across some rising ground from which, in the distance, could be seen the sinister outline of a gibbet. Sharp against the clear morning sky, a grisly trophy hung from it.

"Soldiers," said the man, "is either good or bad. They goes up, or they goes down. If you goes up – the right way mind, not like that fellow there – you might become a general. But if you goes down you finishes up crows' meat, like that fellow there, as you might say."

William said he had every intention of becoming a general.

"I've no doubt you will, young Master, no doubt at all. You'll go far, if you don't go and get yourself killed first. There's too many wars these days for comfortable soldiering!"

The remark caused William to think, and rather cast a pall over the proceedings for several miles. He began to see new possibilities, other than those romantic notions which had coloured his childhood. Those "roaring cannons" could maim and kill.

When the coach, which had been increasingly impeded in its progress by flocks of sheep, carriages, cattle and the milling throng which pulsates

*The Bull and Mouth, Regent Circus, Piccadilly, 1829.*

about a metropolis, finally pulled up at the great posting office by "The Bull and Mouth" in London's Charing Cross, William's young eyes were fairly starting from his head. The rushing wheels had induced a stupor; the teeming carriages, coaches, drays and wagons; the horses, ostlers, coachmen and people, the paupers and the gentry, the tradesmen, soldiery, pickpockets, fine ladies and bawds; the panorama was wonder enough for the seasoned traveller. For the lad from Paxham Village it was overwhelming.

The beaver-hatted gentleman's kindness belied his general air of pessimism. No doubt regarding a would-be soldier sent on his way by a lordship as something of a curiosity, he took William into the hostelry and regaled him with a large slice of pasty and a glass of small ale. Then, having ascertained from the potman that the Colchester post would not depart for another three hours, he became involved in an energetic discussion upon the merits of two racehorses with a neighbour, and promptly forgot all about his young companion. William devoured his pasty, observed the situation, and sought the fresh air.

He looked about in amazement. The buildings towered over his head. There was no horizon, and a murky heat-haze hung like a yellow pall across the sky. The hurry and bustle mystified a country lad. What could

*Soho Square today, where William realised what might have been.*

there be of urgency in a place like this? Could there be somewhere hidden a herd of cows in calf, or a mare to foal, eggs to gather or turnips to pull? William thought not. Could they all be hurrying to their dinners? Surely it lacked at least a full hour to any repast that he knew. This rushing hither and thither must be an alien habit in which London folk alone indulged.

He hastened through the press, assailed by street-sellers. "Buy a toffee apple, young master!" "Peg dolls two for a penny!" "Hot Pies!" In and out of carts and carriages he wove, pausing wide-eyed to observe the be-satinned and wigged gentry. Thus, jostled like a troutlet in a rock-strewn shallow, he came at last into the green comparative solitude of Soho Square.

Even there he was not alone. As he sat down upon a mounting block at the verge wondering whether the time had come to sample Mistress Crackett's pie, he discovered that he was observed. A small boy with a wizened face upon which a large cap with a tassle sat like a tired pudding, stood shivering, hands stuffed for warmth into his tattered sleeves, in spite of the sunshine.

"Spare me a crust, Mister – I'm 'ungry."

William left his bundle, with the red kerchief, in the square, thrust it without a word upon the shadow of what he might have become, that he saw there.

He hurried back to the suddenly friendly seeming bustle of the Bull and Mouth, just in time to climb aboard the Colchester coach. The potman had misinformed him, confusing the timetable for Colchester with that of Dorchester. Set tight between two large and warm ladies, inside this time, for Lord Clayburne was not there to ensure the privilege of outside passage, he slept for most of the onward journey.

Not for several weeks was he sufficiently settled in his mind to commence the series of letters to Mr Graves, which the company at Clayburne Hall read and discussed with such interest and amusement.

# China Teapot

"Shall the Mandarin be black, Father?" George Lambert's piping enquiry was almost carried away by the tangy, gusty breeze into the noisy dockland turmoil.

The question worried him, because he had asked everyone he knew, and no-one ever seemed to have actually seen a Chinee in person. Grown-ups were strange and elusive, didn't like being asked questions to which they hadn't the answers, not by children, at any rate. Juvenile curiosity was not to be encouraged. It was cheeky.

So he had gone to the fount of knowledge. It was essential to find out the colour of the strange and exotic creatures he was about to meet.

He addressed his enquiry to Mr Didcot Crawford, B.A., at the Kensington Academy where he attended each day for instruction. To everyone's surprise, and without any preamble, he just put up his hand and waited until the dominie thought fit to interrupt a dry discourse about coal and Newcastle. "Yes Boy", he rasped, peering over his steel rims, "Come along, speak up."

"Are Mandarins black Sir?"

The question took Mr Crawford unawares. He had a liking for doing things by rote, tables, capitals, definitions. He also had a very bald head, buck teeth and a great many years behind him. His temper was sketchy, mainly because his primitive denture interfered with his diet, making him a martyr to indigestion. His information upon contemporary matters tended to be permanently at least a decade behind the times. He still talked of the "New Young Queen".

Now he paused in mid-discourse, directing what he imagined to be his most penetrating glare towards George, who suddenly realising the enormity of his action, coughed apprehensively and waited. He was fortunate. The dyspeptic qualms were passive.

So no flash of lightening ensued, merely a tangible silence. Then Mr Crawford gathered up the skirts of his gown and stooped to the bottom right-hand drawer of his large and sombre pedestal desk. That was where the cane lived, and the class quaked. But Mr Crawford, when he emerged, was seen to be carrying a book, a large one, bursting with close print. Riffling through the pages he stopped at a group of coloured engravings, which George, feeling very important before the whole class, was summoned forward to examine.

The Chinese features depicted, coloured in by a poorly paid spinster who worked by candlelight, were indeterminately brown, for the paper had perished. The figures postured like those on the wallpaper in his great aunt Jemima's house in Clapham. Great Aunt had more to say than Mr Crawford. She remarked that such figures had been much in vogue when she was a gal and produced a book from Ackermann to prove that the Quality still found them desirable. "None of your gimcrack modern nonsense," she said with spirit. She liked things which lasted, but she still failed to tell him what colour was a Chinaman.

George thought the Chinamen resembled the monkeys which climbed upon some of the golden furniture they call French which he saw at Aunt Jemima's. She said the Chinees were tasteful and English, and the monkeys vulgar, which just went to show the incomprehensibility of adult reasoning.

Great Aunt was starched and pomaded, her features blanched with lemon water and rice powder. When she sat stiffly in her wingchair with one bejewelled claw supported on a long, gold-topped and be-tassled stick, she looked, to George, like a monument. But unlike a monument she spoke and gave answers to questions, which most grown-ups, it seemed, had little time to do. Great Aunt always seemed to have time. She waited for people to speak to her, when she was awake. His mother always had so much to say on her own account that you couldn't really converse with her at all.

George knew Great Aunt must be very old because she talked about people in history as if she'd known them personally. There was Charles I, and Marlborough and Catherine the Great. Since she had a strong feeling for the Iron Duke she quite naturally abhorred Napoleon and anything French unless it was aristocratic. She talked in a tremulous, booming falsetto which George, with youthful inconsequence, found endearing, but which struck terror into her household. It seemed to rise from the very bottom of her tightly laced corsage. George was not supposed to mention that, but it had nevertheless been discussed with much interest during extra-curricular interludes at Mr Crawford's.

"Young George," Great Aunt had quavered. "It stands to reason. Ever heard of Thomas Chippendale?" George hadn't, but he was intrigued by the ominous creaking which accompanied any vocal exertion on the part of this most imposing relative.

"Now there was a craftsman," Great Aunt had continued, as if the famous cabinet maker had been her personal familiar. "Did Harewood for the dear Earl. There's a fellow who knew his Chinees, carved them round mirrors all his life." She paused, sniffed, adjusted a ruffle and continued. "They live in Cathay, in pagodas. The monkeys, now, they're French. They do say they were made to guy that Voltaire creature when he hoped for an invitation to the Imperial Court in St Petersburg. Can't trust the Frenchies. Never trust a Frenchman, boy; chop your head off as soon as look at you."

When George enquired further about the head-chopping he was answered with a gentle, contented snore. Why, oh why, should Chinees be English? And if the Chinees were in some way English, why did Great Aunt Jemima say that Chinamen came from Cathay?

Mr Algernon Lambert, George's father, stiff and upright in frocked black beneath his stovepipe beaver, as befitted a wholesale grocer of considerable substance, was unaware of the problems seething in the carriage beside him. He was indeterminately forty, bewhiskered, and much affected by the solid dignity of the rising merchant aristocracy. Today he felt benevolent, well disposed to the world.

A ragged child with an old man's face clamoured barefoot at the wheels – "Spare a copper, Mister!" Mr Lambert flicked a farthing in the general direction of the cry, which ceased in a scuffle, only to start again on the opposite side. This time he raised his stick; it wasn't a question of malice, rich and poor lived in different worlds. Had George been concerned enough to enquire it would have been explained that all the seething raggle-taggle had no responsibility, hence its inconsequence. God looks after the man who has enough money to take care of himself.

"Father – the Mandarin, shall he be black?"

Mr Lambert duly considered his son's question. Due consideration was one of his main characteristics. It gave him a self-confident appearance which had carried him far. When others leapt into the breach without a thought, Mr Lambert considered. Thus he survived where the less cautious were lost. His pronouncements were not weighty, they just seemed to be.

"Black? I should strongly doubt that, son. The Chinese are yellow. They have heathen beliefs like the . . . um . . . Hottentots, but I am informed they display considerably more intelligence than black men. They aren't cannibals, and they drink tea like we do." That at least, thought George, was a comfort, particularly when you were about to meet some of them.

The carriage jogged forward in fits and starts on iron rims over the uneven cobbles. Humanity, wheels, street criers with fly-blown merchandise, colour gyrated in the sunshine. A half-starved cur scampered, tail down, into an alley, dragging a scrag of rotten meat, and a pickpocket, taking advantage of the commotion, skilfully lifted a watch and a fine linen kerchief. The dockside scavengers, human and animal, made holiday with their masters.

On the morning of 3rd September 1849, the tenth anniversary of the birth of Algernon and Melissa Lambert's first son, George, half London seemed to be making its way to the East India docks basin.

"And shall the Mandarin be coming ashore, Father, so that all the people may see him?"

Mr Lambert considered again. Unconsciously his son had recalled a dispute of the night before which he had tried to banish from his mind. Mrs Lambert, Melissa, the ornament of his early nuptial felicity, was the problem. Women were unpredictable. Women changed. That was a matter of masculine common knowledge, but Melissa was becoming socially ambitious. The symptoms had been developing ever since they moved from companionable Brixton to stylish Knightsbridge, and Algernon, who was on the whole a fair man, wondered if he was to blame. His business ventures flourished. It was right that his mode of living should express his prosperity to the world at large, but that his wife should monopolise the conduct of their joint social progress had not been part of his original scheme of things.

Melissa had taken exception to today's outing. It was George's birthday treat, one his father had chosen. George had been the envy of all his colleagues at Mr Crawford's when he announced, following his enquiry as to the colour of mandarins, that the auspicious occasion was to be celebrated by a visit to the Ke-Ying, the first Chinese junk ever to venture into the Atlantic, certainly the first ever to tie up at London Docks, and there was a Mandarin aboard.

England was a land of adventurers and it had been for centuries. The pirates of the Spanish Main, the sea captains and generals, the merchant soldiers of India, had left the legacy of an Empire which dominated the mid-nineteenth century world. The effete aristocracy of history, rich by inheritance and intermarriage, was beginning, albeit reluctantly, to accept into its ranks the new fortune-making merchants. Horizons were ever wider, embracing in all directions fresh opportunities for exploration and conquest, first by the adventurers, then the missionaries, and finally the businessmen.

Thus the interest in strange, foreign things was intense, particularly for the men, who sought always a new challenge. Their womenfolk, on the other hand, the wives of the successful at least, were sated with the extrovert benefits of their husbands' lucrative activities. Most of them were the product of a sheltered upbringing, tutored at home in the gentle domestic arts by impoverished spinsters and university men steeped in 18th century tradition. They held court in various degrees of grandeur, reflecting the prosperity, or otherwise, of the men. In their little domains they commanded an hierarchy of domestics, thriving on the petty disputes of neighbourly competition. They shared little of their husbands' ambitions, and anything which did not further the current fad in social advancement was not likely to find favour with the lady of the house.

Mrs Lambert considered the excursion to the Ke-Ying too anonymous. It did nothing to advance her prestige. She would have preferred a reception at home, something to impress the neighbours.

"Lambert," she announced, with the pointed disregard for her husband's friendly overtures throughout dinner which heralded an argument, "I believe it unwise for poor George to visit this foreign ship. Who knows what poisonous vapours there may not be aboard a heathen vessel. You know the boy is frail; what if he takes the plague? Mrs Prendergast says . . ."

That particular remark of the redoubtable Mrs Prendergast, the large wife of a successful neighbouring jeweller, who by constant repetition of wise saws, and the bestowal of condescending attention upon the younger matrons, had achieved ascendancy in the local clique, was never recounted. Mention of this formidable lady, and the tinkling of the newly purchased piano-forte, produced in Mr Lambert a condition of near apoplexy.

"Bother Mrs Prendergast," he said, expelling his breath slowly in an effort to maintain a certain domestic equilibrium before the servants. "One day George shall inherit my position, Melissa, and to have met a Chinee shall surely broaden his experience. You mollycoddle the boy!" Quite how the meeting with a Chinaman might benefit a prospective wholesale grocer, Mr Lambert was not clear, but he did derive some small satisfaction from the personal assertion, even though an uncomfortable awareness of the defensive nature of his argument made him writhe inwardly.

"But Algernon, my dear," protested Mrs Lambert, resorting to first names in a misguided assumption that her husband might be chivvied into agreement by resolute, personal nagging, "Mrs Prendergast . . ."

Mrs Prendergast was consigned very shortly to the devil. Melissa sniffed piteously into a tiny square of lacey cambric, and when a tentative resumption of protest elicited only a thunderous declaration from her husband that he would "hear no more", she retired to her piano-forte. Thence there soon welled dolorously the harmonies of a study by Mr Chopin, played with great deliberation, but with no effect whatsoever, since Mr Lambert, apart from hating the piano-forte, was also tone-deaf. He wished heartily for a return to the days of his youth when, before the general availability of what many regarded as mechanical music, ladies were content to sing to their own accompaniment. A guitar he could have silenced, he could have thrown it out of the window, even broken its neck. The piano-forte in his salon, the best from Waring and Gillow, was somewhat robust. It would defy attack!

So the tinkling chords continued monotonously. He clapped his hands over his ears and endeavoured to concentrate. He had a pamphlet before him on the table, a pamphlet brought back from the docks the previous day by the clerk he had charged with the arrangements for today's outing.

Not only was he enthusiastic on his master's behalf, but he was also personally interested. Enoch Jones was, as his name implied, Welsh; he was also young and ambitious, keen to impress, and anxious to report news of his rising fortunes back to those contemporaries of his in the Valleys who, not having the courage to launch themselves into the wide world, had scoffed at his ambitions. "Funny people," he rehearsed. "Eatin' birds' nests an' all yellow-like. They'd chop you up an' eat you as soon as dammit."

Enoch had been told to carry a message to Captain Kellett so that Mr Lambert would be shown directly aboard the Ke-Ying without having to wait in a long and tedious queue. He had done more. He wanted to participate in any outcome of Mr Lambert's adventure. He sensed that there was more to it than a frivolous outing for the day.

Adopting an air suitable to what he regarded as his first responsible mission, he had confronted a Chinaman who stood at the top of the gangway and demanded instant audience with the part owner and Master of the Ke-Ying in person.

As a consequence of his clerk's diligence, Mr Lambert had before him not only a pamphlet with a rather smudged image of a Chinese junk on the cover, but also a sheet of closely written and neatly tabulated notes pinned to it.

At that point Mr Lambert's resolve wavered. Should he, like Melissa, be worrying about the plague? He hoped Enoch's enthusiasm had not overtaken his common sense, his ability to observe and consider. There had been an outbreak of Plague in the City only recently. Wasn't that enough to create apprehension in view of those rumoured cases reported from

Whitechapel? Were they only rumour, or could an infection really have come from China?

Algernon Lambert may have been a stolid English businessman, but there were stories abroad and he wasn't devoid of imagination.

He'd heard that the symptoms of Plague were horrifying. What had the old General said, at the Club?

"Saw it in Seringapatam, Lambert. Terrible. Lucky none of our people got it.

"Three days, that's all. couldn't eat or drink a thing. Boils all over. Couldn't breathe. Just turned blue. Bleeding no good, nor leeches. People tried 'em just got infected too. Whole villages wiped out, people, animals, everything."

Well, what if such a scourge came to Knightsbridge? Perversely, he smiled; might thin the neighbours out a little; unworthy thought.

Number 2, Draycott Square was a substantial dwelling, but it was no palace, no location for a new Decameron. A new edition of the Bocaccio classic, with illustrations, was currently circulating in the City. The Decameron – even a Pentameron or Duomeron – of Lambertaccio. Mr Lambert smiled again in spite of the tinkling piano-forte.

A Knightsbridge refuge from the Plague Terror, with all the license of Bocaccio. Time was when the thought of Melissa as companion in an isolated idyll would have offered prospects of almost unbearable delight. Now, in the unlikely event of such an occurrence it would be his fortune to find the ubiquitous and nauseating Mrs Perndergast among the company in his haven. The piano-forte, with the impact of an elusive itch finally scratched, halted on a tentative discord. He lost himself in the Ke-Ying's odyssey.

"Shall the Mandarin be coming ashore, Father?"

Mr Lambert returned to the present.

"For the time being, son, the Mandarin will stay in the house which was built specially for him on the deck of the Ke-Ying. He and all his Chinee companions must remain on board until the Authorities, in their wisdom, are quite certain they do not carry the plague. Since the English sailors have been allowed ashore for several weeks that seems a little unreasonable to me. Most likely the disease comes, not from China, but with our soldiers returning from the Indies. There has, as far as we know, been no outbreak of the pestilence at any of the other places the ship visited. That was one of the things I asked Mr Jones to discover for me."

With that lengthy speech Mr Lambert finally convinced himself. He dismissed Melissa's social antics, cast aside the lingering annoyance of her icy breakfast hauteur. He was looking forward to the day's outing. George never forgot it.

"In any case," continued Mr Lambert after a pause, during which the carriage did not progress very far but the turmoil round about increased. They were passing other ships now, vessels from all over the world, blown here by winds from every quarter, fair and foul, icy cold and torridly warm, to disgorge their cargo into the ever-hungry maw of London's trade. This was the heart of an expanding Empire. "In any case, those Chinamen have been at sea far too long to carry an infection."

"How long have they been, Father?"

Mr Lambert had found the pamphlet absorbing. Enoch Jones's notes gave substance to its romance. Enoch knew that Captain Kellett was more than a mere adventurer, that in addition to the travelling exhibition of curiosities which he had piloted half way round the world, he also carried full powers to negotiate on behalf of certain merchants already trading in and around the China Seas.

He had carried letters which preceded him direct from St Helena, and these, listing mouth-watering prices for tea, ginger and spices, for gums and lacquers, even perfumes, had appealed to Enoch as much as to his employer. There were those, it seemed, who were making a fortune selling drugs. The Chinese, he'd heard, smoked opium like tobacco.

Thus Mr Lambert had lingered long in his study that night. One of the letters which had lain on his desk for six months and more contained a memorable passage.

"So, my friend, our affairs prosper vastly here. It's true we must take account of many strange heathen customs and habits and some of our people are not of the most patient. I am certain, nevertheless, that with an intelligent application and a recognition of the disadvantages suffered by those not so fortunate as to be born British we can build up a trade restricted only by the number of ships we can find to carry our merchandise.

"Our past associations have always been to mutual advantage. Could we not resume a partnership? There is plenty here for all, a fortune for a dozen of us if you wish, and no great hardship beyond those entailed by a few short months at sea."

Mr Lambert had a sudden vision of a long, long road winding far over water and land, straight to the romantic East. Only one obstacle stood in the way. Between him and a brilliant sunrise lay a vast piano-forte. He shook away the vision, only to find that Enoch's comments kept returning to his mind. With difficulty he forced himself back to the present. This was George's birthday. He must consider the entertainment of his son and heir.

"They've come a long, long way, George, and they had quite a lot of adventures. First the ship had to sail from Canton to Hong Kong. You see,

*The Ke-Ying.*

after Captain Kellett, who first had the notion to sail a Chinese junk to Europe, had bought her, the Chinese decided that they did not want a vessel of the Celestial Chinese Merchant Fleet, particularly a grand old veteran already a hundred years old, sailing off among us white devils, so he had to pretend he was only bound for Hong Kong."

Mr Lambert took a silver case from an inner pocket, extracted a cheroot and proceeded to light it with a sulphur match. George watched the operation with remote interest. He knew his father wouldn't continue until it was fully alight. His imagination seethed with visions of ancient, posturing, slant-eyed Orientals, hanging like monkeys from the rigging of a huge golden vessel with tiers of slender oars like the Argo, about which he had been told by Mr Crawford, and rows of cannon and masts like the Victory, of which he had learned from his Great Aunt. Canton, Hong Kong, the exotic names made strange harmony. He wished Great Aunt Jemima had stayed awake longer, she was so much easier to question than his father. "Is Hong Kong in Cathay?" he enquired.

"Er . . . yes, I suppose so, George. They call it China now, though."

"So what did Captain Kellett do when he got to Hong Kong?"

The cheroot glowed.

*Saloon of the Ke–Ying*

"First he bribed an official not to disclose his intention. It must have been obvious from the supplies that he took on board that he had a considerable voyage in mind. Then he slipped anchor at dead of night, having signified to the Authorities that he would not be sailing for a week.

"The Ke-Ying rounded the Cape of Good Hope and made St Helena, across the Pacific Ocean, in a little over three months. The English sailors wanted to call a halt there, in fact there was nearly a mutiny because of the strange behaviour of the Chinese crew. I was reading about it last night in Mr Jones's notes. If there was a storm they followed their practice just as if they were still coasting off China. They tied bits of red rag and ribands to everything, set off fire-crackers and retired below, leaving all the work to the English, who weren't at all happy. For months they had been increasingly impatient with the heathen behaviour of the natives.

"Why did the Chinamen behave so strangely?"

"They're strange people, Son. Suppose they meant to scare the sea spirits away. They're terribly superstitious. Didn't even trust the English compass at first. Then, when they discovered that it really worked, they thought it was magic and concluded that they had to pacify it?"

"How would they pacify a compass, Father?"

"Well, they had to give it something they particularly liked themselves, and their favourite food is pork! They left a meal of stewed pickled pork on the binnacle for it every night!"

"What happened when they found that the compass couldn't eat it?"

"Ah, well –. They never did find out because the English first watch got into the habit of eating stewed pork at midnight. And that, I suppose, was when more trouble started, because someone dropped a knife into the apparatus near the needle, and that set the ship off course! That's probably why the voyage took so long.

"It must have been difficult for the Captain, having a mutinous crew. The Ke-Ying isn't an ordinary ship and I should imagine her odd ways take a lot of learning. The Captain didn't want to have to break in an entirely new crew, not for the few weeks it should take to reach England.

Although the Island Magistrate was sympathetic it took a great deal of argument to persuade the Englishmen to stay with their eccentric ship, but in the end they were convinced that with such a short distance still to go, they might as well remain to journey's end. Their conclusion might have been different had they foreseen the adventures yet to come! As for the Chinamen, I don't suppose they understood what was happening in any case!"

"Did they come straight home from St Helena?" George thought they'd taken a long time to reach London. Great Aunt had had a cousin in the garrison when Napoleon was exiled there, and correspondence with him, she had said, had taken but a few days to arrive.

"Oh yes, George," said Mr Lambert, "that was the intention. That should have been the end of the journey – but don't forget that knife in the compass.

"Captain Kellett did set sail for England and home, but he ran into contrary winds and great storms, and Chinese junks are not very manageable in deep water. It took three whole months to beat up the South Atlantic and there was a great deal of trouble with that mixed company, only twelve Englishmen, remember, to thirty heathens, whose notions of navigation in deep water didn't improve one wit. At long last they did sight land, but it wasn't the land they'd expected. They sailed, not up the Thames to London, but up Long Island Sound, to New York!"

George in his turn considered. Then he counted on his fingers.

"So they were six months getting to America?"

Mr Lambert now had the printed pamphlet open in his hand. The Ke-Ying's itinerary had assumed complications beyond even his retentive memory.

"That's correct, George, and they still had a long way to go. However, they made good use of their time while they put everything on the ship in

*After deck of the Ke–Ying, showing He–Sing's quarters.*

order, and crowds started coming to see the result when they had finished. They came to look at He-Sing the Mandarin, and Sam-Sing the artist, who painted and sold them pictures, and they made a great deal of money. After that the Ke-Ying sailed for a successful visit to Boston, and only in February of this year, eight months after reaching America, and fourteen from Hong Kong, did they set out upon the most dramatic part of the journey, the last leg to England."

Mr Lambert turned a page.

"That last leg must have been exciting! They ran into a hurricane five days out. The sails split – they are only made of matting – and a huge rudder rope that runs right under the ship, broke. But do you know, that old vessel remaïned steady and they hardly took in any water at all? They made the crossing of the Atlantic in twenty-one days, that's faster than most clippers. They put in at the Island of Jersey first, and although nobody is inclined to believe the story, they do say it's all written in the Captain's log, so we shall be able to read it for ourselves."

The carriage had stopped. " 'Ere y'are!" shouted the driver. "Ve Ke-Ying as ever vos, all the vay from China!"

As the Lamberts got down the turmoil enveloped young George. Urchins dashed in and out among the gaping crowd. Shouts from rigging, high up, rasp of block and tackle, smell of horses, river sewage, warm serge. George thought he sniffed frying pork and burnt sugar.

To a small boy the Ke-Ying was overwhelming. 160 feet long, she towered ninety feet to the top of her naturally curved mainmast, high into the brittle May morning. She was fashioned not as an English ship, from timbers moulded and worked by men, but rather from wood which had grown naturally misshapen and then been adapted to make part of the remarkable hull. It was an edifice rather than a construction, a large mass of man-made fantasy, strayed into the down-to-earth realism of London.

"You see that, George," exclaimed Mr Lambert. "See how that timber's formed. It must have been ancient when they cut it. Look at the size of the rudder!" And he pointed to the cumbersome twenty-four foot, postless device which had directed the lumbering craft more than halfway round the world. "And look George, they've painted eyes on the prow so that the ship may see where she's going!" Mr. Lambert was enjoying himself.

Captain Kellett had been well briefed upon his visitor. Mr Lambert, he knew, might well be persuaded to invest in a large cargo of merchandise from China. He stood at attention, in braided blue, bearded, and with a

*A contemporary cartoon. The English public crowd to see the junk.*

twinkle in his eye, at the top of the gangway to greet his visitors. On his right was He-Sing, Mandarin, fifth grade, by the crystal button on his round hat, while on his left stood Sam-Sing the artist, with no button, but a smile which split his leathery, ageless face from ear to ear.

"Welcome aboard, Mr Lambert," said the Captain. "Welly Welcome" said Sam-Sing and He-Sing together, bowing with their hands folded inside the deep loose sleeves of their silken, colourful robes. George would never believe a wallpaper picture again. Chinamen, he decided, didn't even begin to look like thc pictures in the book! His father was right, they were yellow, and not at all frightening.

George Lambert's birthday treat now began in earnest. As he mounted the gangway he could hear the river lapping gently between the stone dock and the towering timber. On deck, shaking hands with the great, bluff Captain and being greeted by the elegant Chinese, he entered a world of pure magic. In his mind he rehearsed already the wonders he would recount to his classmates and Great Aunt Jemima. The members of the public, paying over their pennies at the top of the gangway, streamed by, turning the pages of their pamphlets to find clarification of the mysteries on display, the cannon, the open kitchen, the house of the Mandarin, the water tanks, the Chinese sailors themselves, and here he was, George Lambert, come aboard as the personal guest of the Captain!

There seemed to be a great deal of kow-towing, which Captain Kellett endeavoured to explain. Only recently, it appeared, during a tour by the Lord Mayor, Sam-Sing and He-Sing had been with difficulty restrained from according the braided State Footmen more courtesies than the guest of honour because of the greater embellishment of their livery. Here now were two more perfectly unremarkable beings to be feted.

George stood wide-eyed, not knowing where to turn, until Sam-Sing, with an artist's sensibility, noticed the young visitor's confusion. With quiet dignity he beckoned, guiding him aft in the wake of the Captain and Mr Lambert, already deep in conversation. He-Sing led the way to the small elaborately carved superstructure where he lived beneath the towering, balconied stern while Captain Kellett translated the huge letters displayed there. They besought the waters, he said, not to enter the ship.

At last, passing below into the Stateroom they were seated at a long low table on carved, upright blackwood stools. "Well, what do you think of her, Mr Lambert?" asked the Captain. "Rather special, don't you think?"

The ship's Joss, a small, brilliantly gilded, Buddha-like figure, smiled down from a carved shrine at the end of what was almost a ceremonial chamber, certainly not a cabin. There were cabinets of curiosities, opium pipes, vases, candlesticks and strangely fashioned vessels.

*Portrait of He—Sing by Sam Sing from documents kept by George Lambert to celebrate his son's birthday.*

"The Joss is called Chin-Tee," announced the Captain. "He's our patron. Looks after the ship, you know. Ask He-Sing. Actually he's done us pretty well. One way and another this has been a queer trip altogether, and I can't pretend I'm not relieved to be safe back in London.

"Of course, the hazards we've survived would never threaten our normal deep-sea packets. This craft was really only built for inshore

*Stern of the Ke–Ying, showing the great rudder.*

waters, and we've sailed more miles in her than would circumnavigate the globe. Quite an accomplishment for a craft built in 1750, don't you think?"

"Remarkable, remarkable," was Mr Lambert's only comment.

"Sam-Sing did all this, the paintings and the carved flowers and dragons," continued the Captain, waving an all-embracing arm at the elaborate decorations as the visitors looked about in wonder.

"We've probably done the old tub a good turn. There's been a typhoon in Hong Kong, I hear, and they say a great many of the junks in harbour were completely wrecked. A thousand and more of the people living in them perished too, so they say, drowned by a tidal wave. If we hadn't left when we did, perhaps we shouldn't be here to tell the tale at all."

When the two men began to discuss business, George went on deck with Sam-Sing and watched while he drew pictures for the visitors. He worked with a series of brushes, producing his Chinese likenesses with deft, delicate strokes, tinting them with watercolour. During a pause he produced two portraits for George, signing them with both Chinese and European characters.

Time passed quickly. When he had tired of watching the artist at work, George observed the traffic on the tideway. Sailing barges, rowing boats of all sizes, pinnaces, horsedrawn vessels by the towpath. London, it was said, drew her breath by the river and the pattern of new interest changed by the minute.

George was surprised when Sam-Sing put away his brushes. "That enough for day," he said, shutting his cash box. "We go b'low take cha with Captain. You like cha?"

"Oh yes, if you please, sir," replied George, his mind seething with the happenings of a remarkable day. The boys at Mr Crawford's Academy would never believe it. Whatever cha was, he was going to have some.

The Captain and Mr Lambert still sat in the Stateroom. Their heads were close together and pens and paper were on the table.

"Ah, young Master George," said the Captain. "One must, I believe, wish you a happy birthday. I suppose the boy takes tea, sir?"

The tea which, disappointedly, George realised was what the Chinees called cha, was brought by three of the native sailors. The Mandarin and the artist each received their own small porcelain pot, and they sipped noisily from tiny, fragile bowls.

For the Captain and his visitors there was placed on the table a fine service of silver and some of the new porcelain cups with handles. There was also a plate of small cakes, some biscuits and a dish of sugar sweets. The Captain set about pouring. "I never thought of asking, Mr Lambert.

Would you prefer China? I always take Indian – or perhaps you'd like ale?"

"No, no, Captain," said Mr Lambert. "Indian will do very well. That's a very handsome tea service."

"I thought so, Mr Lambert," said the Captain, holding up the teapot. "A little old-fashioned, perhaps, because it's silver, and all the ladies say that porcelain's the thing now. Still, as you see," and he waved his free arm at the decor, "I'm scarcely a man for modish fancies."

Algernon Lambert mentally recoiled, wondering if his liking for the tea-service was a "modish fancy". He liked it. The delicately chased silver pot with slightly canted sides and that curious little finial, looked feminine somehow, and in the prevailing context of convoluted gilt and blackwood, lonely. He could afford to gratify his desires, but wasn't it silly to want a teapot, particularly one that wasn't for sale?

As he concluded that here might be the ideal gift for Melissa he realised that he had fallen rudely silent in his host's presence and that the Captain was regarding him curiously.

"Would you consider selling the tea service?"

"I hadn't really thought about it," said the Captain, "I keep it as, well, a kind of souvenir of the young fellow I bought it from in Boston, Fibb his name was. He stopped an urchin picking my pocket down on the waterfront one night and we became quite friendly. He took me home and introduced me to his elderly mother, an Italian lady.

"Fibb's father had been a soldier who came from Paxham in Kent. He met his wife in the Italian War. The couple were about to leave Boston to trek West where there was fine land to be had just for the claiming. The old lady didn't want to sell the tea service, but the boy said they needed the money to buy what he called their "outfit". Everyone seemed to be moving westward after either land or gold, and prospects were good – if you survived attack by the Red Indians. Another fertile field for fortune hunters," and he added hurriedly, suddenly realising that he was distracting a possible client, "But no wit as rich as China!"

In the event Captain Kellett proved to be no more possessive of the silver tea service than the young American hopefully travelling West. He had the packing case that had been made for it fetched from his cabin. Then he went on to talk earnestly about shipping rice in ballast, quantities, prices.

The atmosphere in the stateroom was oppressive. A thread of pale blue exotic smoke threaded up from beneath the grinning Joss. Overhead the solid old oriental timbers echoed to the hard shuffling footsteps of the apparently endless procession of sightseers.

The talk went on and the Chinamen retired. George felt drowsy. There were figures discussed. He heard Hong Kong mentioned and Foochow, Shanghai, Amoy, Ning-Po and Canton. There were tonnages and dates, and large sums of money.

The hard edge of the wooden seat cut the back of his legs. The shuffling overhead diminished, became spasmodic and stopped. A suggestion of incense drifted from somewhere in the bowels of the ship. This was a fairy tale and he was under a spell; then he heard hoof beats and the hard edge had been replaced by horsehair. He was in a moving vehicle, people were talking.

He awoke to daylight in his own room and if he hadn't seen the two little paintings by Sam-Sing and a small pamphlet with the Ke-Ying on the cover lying at his bedside, the whole episode might have been a dream. For the moment he was unable to explain the folded paper propped behind the candle.

Mr Lambert, sitting beside his sleeping son in the carriage, went home in a haze of a different kind. Captain Kellett had opened up so many beckoning horizons that his mind was in a whirl. Even his habitual consideration was stirred. His self-satisfied suburban existence suddenly seemed pointless. He had a good chief clerk who could well look after his warehouses. The ghost of the faraway exotic smell which permeated the timbers of the Ke-Ying lingered in his nostrils. He would start a new venture, he would take a leaf from Captain Kellett's book, not physically perhaps, but he would invest in a cargo. He would write to his old friend. Already he saw himself at Lloyds, looking in The Times for sailings and arrivals, harking for the Lutine bell, hurrying down to the docks to inspect his cargoes.

An intriguing prospect, but one he would have to break gently to Melissa. She didn't like change, didn't care for business at all, although she wasn't averse to the acceptance of its proceeds. He had been short with her of late. Perhaps he should have been more willing to realise that as the mistress of a new establishment in Knightsbridge she had certain responsibilities, certain standards to maintain, if only to impress the neighbours. A pity they were so impressive themselves. It made her so demanding.

Algernon thought of Melissa. She'd been very pretty, blue eyes, flaxen hair, tripping lightly on a Summer's morn across the lawn of a neighbour's garden. A neighbour; how he had put himself about to cultivate the elderly impecunious Colonel, sat for hours listening to tales of campaigns which lost themselves in whiskery choleric enthusiasm. The Colonel had political opinions too, which Algernon, desperate for even a fleeting glimpse of the delightful creature who monopolised his waking thoughts to the exclusion of all else, had to endure.

Fifteen years had passed since the son of a successful businessman with

*St Matthews Church, Brixton, where George Lambert married Melissa.*

prospects courted the daughter of a retired Officer of the Foot Guards who lived on Brixton Hill. It had seemed such a romantic place, where the Effra flowed in a riot of luxurious woodland by the side of the road.

They had met with increasing frequency throughout one all too short but glorious Summer. In the Autumn, he remembered wryly, he had actually had the temerity to kiss her behind the woodshed. She made no protest.

There came that significant Sunday when the elderly cousin came to visit. In spite of his mother's objections on the basis of Sabbath sanctity, an expedition in the carriage with Melissa, and of course the elderly relative as chaperone, was reluctantly condoned.

They set forth toward Norwood, talking stiltedly of the weather and other such mundane subjects which the presence of a rather prim and elderly lady constrained.

At the bottom of Norwood Hill, just by the Gipsy Tavern, the warmth of the day and the motion of the carriage, had their way. The escort dozed, snoring peacefully, steel-rimmed spectacles askew upon her gently perspiring button of a nose.

The young couple silently got down and sauntered into the woods. "Tell your fortune Dearie?"

She came from nowhere, a colourful, comfortable Gipsy lady in black set off with a great crisp white apron, a red kerchief at her throat, and heavy golden ear-rings. Her jet hair too was bound in scarlet. She turned moist, deep, dark eyes upon Algernon. "Pretty, very pretty, Sir. Cross me palm with silver, Master, an' I'll tell the pretty lady's fortune."

For sixpence Algernon Lambert's fate was sealed. For him, said the Gipsy, with his kind face, a prosperous future. He admired his "kind face" in the mirror that night, when he couldn't sleep for the thought of Melissa. For the pretty lady there was soon to be a handsome husband.

They were married at St Matthews, an imposing church at the bottom of Brixton Hill, with parental blessings from both sides. The Colonel, peppery as ever, went to meet his Commanding Officer in the Sky very soon after.

Not for the first time, romance was fickle. Conflicting domestic and commercial interests soon clouded the first blissful glow, the mirage, of marital bliss. Melissa became immersed in her ceaseless round of entertainments. Algernon's business, advancing from strength to strength, provided refuge from a home in which he was daily made to feel more of a stranger.

Nevertheless, he would make one more effort. He hadn't forgotten the day on Norwood Hill. On his lap in the carriage was a parcel, carefully wrapped by one of the Ke-Ying's Chinese sailors. It contained the case with the silver tea service in it. He would start a new era, be more diplomatic. George should not witness endless parental bickering. He would present the silver to Melissa as a peace offering. She had said she wanted a small tea service for intimate entertaining, apart from the massive affair over which she presided at her evenings and at homes. As his son dozed, he rehearsed the presentation.

Alas for his resolutions.

"You look ill, George," Melissa fussed, as soon as the birthday pair came through the door. "Lambert, you shouldn't have taken him. I told you you shouldn't. Straight up to bed with you, George, and you shall take a dose of physic before you sleep."

"Melissa," said Algernon, pacifically. "I've brought you a little present, something I think you'll like," and he handed her the parcel.

"You choose the most inconvenient moments, Lambert," said Melissa. "You know it's one of my musical evenings and I must have everything prepared before Mrs Prendergast gets here. What is it?"

Algernon stifled his instinctive wish to consign Mrs Prendergast to perdition. "It's a silver tea set, Melissa, one that Captain Kellett got in America."

Melissa had no time for personal niceties. She rode high on her social hobby horse.

"You are too tiresome, Lambert," she said. "You know very well I didn't want silver, all the best people are buying china now. Why couldn't you get me something by Mr Spode? You can use that for both China and India tea."

Her husband stood stock still as she swept toward the salon, dispelling as she hurried, thoughtless, back to her familiars, not only a lingering vision of a beautiful young girl on Norwood Hill, but also any hope of the reconciliation Algernon had planned on the way home.

There were many coats hanging in the cloak room, and a maid, whose name he didn't even know, hovered to take his things. From behind the double arched door which led into the salon of his – yes, his – house, there drifted the tinkling of the piano-forte, accompanied now by the scraping of a fiddle. A rising swell of feminine chatter flowed through the brief opening and enveloped his wife. This time Algernon Lambert did not consider at all.

He went up to his room, the master bedroom they called it, and hurriedly packed a single bag. Shortly afterwards, having quietly left a note by his son's bed, he crept out of the house.

He took a carriage to Clapham, impatient with the driver's insistence on making a wide detour to avoid any possible contact with North Kennington where the cholera was rife. Arriving at last, he remained closeted with Aunt Jemima for an hour. She did not fall asleep, and as her nephew departed there was a touch of a gladiatorial salute about the jewelled hand raised briefly in farewell.

Algernon then proceeded to Brixton where he spent the night at the home of a certain young widow of his acquaintance. He left her the teaset as a keepsake. She was delighted but tearful.

He wasn't at his office on the following day. Neither did Enoch Jones take his seat at the tall pulpit-like contrivance by the door in the clerks' room. The Managing Clerk consulted a memorandum delivered by hand later in the morning, shook his head and sat for several minutes, pondering. The staff watched him in various degrees of feigned preoccupation. They sensed a momentous occasion.

A bluebottle buzzed against a window and from below there drifted the sounds of people, of horses, and wheels. The life of London went on.

At last, when the tension had come to the verge of bursting point the Managing Clerk stood up, summoned two juniors, and to the astonishment of everyone, took up a bundle of files, gathered a number of loose letters upon which he had been working, and walked resolutely into the office of his Principal.

Later in the day, fingering his cravat, top-hatted and carrying a case, but still without a word to anyone, he travelled to Knightsbridge. Mrs Lambert was unwilling to receive him since she was taking tea with Mrs Prendergast.

When the Managing Clerk, having waited for over an hour, finally sat down in her presence she was haughtily impatient, not even offering him refreshment. His attempt to soften the blow by reporting the facts in his own terms met with imperious incredibility. "Don't speak such nonsense. I don't believe a word!"

So he produced the memorandum.

Long after the messenger had gone Melissa still sat, staring into space. Then she wept, but not bitterly. It is not so hard to be resigned when you've been given a house and a handsome allowance, and you weren't likely to be troubled, ever again, by tiresome business matters. Mrs Prendergast agreed entirely.

Neither Melissa nor any of Algernon Lambert's acquaintances in London ever saw him again.

# Sovereign Teapot

Regent Street, decided Alice Burrows, turning south in the early Autumn sunlight, was not improved by the removal of the colonnade. Alice liked grandeur, and those towering columns had certainly been grand. They made you feel like a somebody and without them the street seemed wider, emptier. It still had an impressive sweep, but those old pillars had related somehow with the puny humans marching below them. Now one moved in space.

All this modernisation, this improvement, may be for the best, thought Alice, as indeed the dear Queen had pronounced before subsiding into what appeared to be a state of perpetual mourning, but she wasn't quite sure. Wasn't the Queen taking things a little too seriously? Didn't she know other people felt lonely? Didn't all those courtiers and politicians and ambassadors make a difference? Alice had no courtiers and she really felt the need for company.

New things were arriving all the time. She liked new and surprising developments, but if they were too drastic they were upsetting. Change was acceptable, providing the background remained stable. So if the pillars had remained, would she, Alice, have felt any less lonely?

She carried her forty-odd summers lightly. She felt attractive in well-fitted dark blue bombazine surmounted by a fetching little pelisse trimmed with white fur. August 1870, like many other English Augusts, had almost abandoned its late summer pretence, and although the sun shone briskly enough, it tended to be chilly.

The striking, contented features were set off by a smart bonnet straight out of the latest Journal des Modes. Dressmaking and millinery were hobbies, that particular publication almost a standard work of reference.

Not that she always agreed with it. Recently she had noticed an alarming tendency to refer to the "older matron". Did this, she wondered, refer to her? Or was it merely the rambling of a young editor, or editress, surely, finding his – or her, feet. She certainly didn't feel matronly.

*Old Regent Street looking towards the quadrant.*

The last issue of the Journal had provided food for thought. It announced the discovery of a new "tournure", a physical appendage called a "bombe", which, worn in the appropriate manner, would emphasise those feminine attributes which attracted the male. That was what the journalist said. Alice bought a pair, spent some time in front of her cheval mirror, and decided that she hadn't yet attained a condition of Hogarthian decrepitude. She didn't yet require false physical replacements like the aged figure in the famous print. She hid them away, preferring the suggested alternative, embellishment rather than exaggeration. Fully aware of her continuing charms, she advanced with conscious elegance inside her fashionable bustle. In Argyll Street she stopped before the Palais Royal.

Sideshows and exhibitions fascinated her. The Crystal Palace in Hyde Park, opened two years after Algernon Lambert performed the second male exodus of her life – Mr Burrows had merely departed in a perfectly conventional coffin following a fever – had given her the flavour. She now annually purchased a season ticket which entitled her to visit the kaleidoscopic series of events in the redesigned glass extravaganza at Sydenham. The band concerts, circuses, the balloon ascents, exhibitions and fireworks, even the sporting events, provided a constant source of amusement; they also gave her a vested interest in any out-of-the-ordinary display.

# TRADE MARK IZOD'S PATENT CORSETS. TRADE MARK

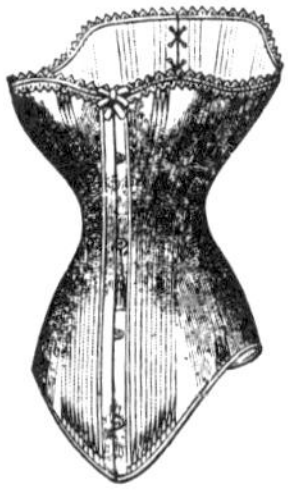

Upon the shape of the Corset entirely depends the accurate fit of a Lady's Dress or Costume.

The Patent Corsets of Messrs. Izod & Son are cut in exquisite proportions, made of the best materials, and finished by their Patent Steam-moulding Process, so that the fabric and bones are adapted with marvellous accuracy to every curve and undulation of the finest type of figure. These Corsets also give great support, and they fit so accurately and comfortably that a very small size can be worn without the slightest injury to the figure.

The variations in fashion are vigilantly watched and every necessary alteration is made to adapt these Corsets to the prevailing style of dress.

The quality of the materials used, and the accuracy in fit of each Corset, is maintained through every change of fashion.

The Patentees desire to call special attention to their Trade Mark.

These Corsets may be had of all respectable Drapers and Ladies' Outfitters, at various prices, and in a variety of material— viz, Coutill, Single and Double; White, Dove and Grey, Scarlet Lastings, Black Italian Cloths.

They are made with either Plain or Pear Shaped Busks.

The Belted Corset is also produced.

IZOD'S PATENT MOULDED TRADE MARK. SEWN CORSETS.

*Only such Corsets as bear our Trade Mark Stamped on them are Genuine and Warranted.*

"The Steam-moulded Corsets of Messrs. Izod & Son have obtained a justly-merited place in public estimation. These Corsets are composed of the best materials, are cut in exquisite proportion, are finished by steam-moulding, and are acknowledged model types of female form. Thus manufactured, it is by no means surprising that the feminine portion of the public inquire for the admirable Corsets of Draper and Milliner, and that the demand for these Corsets is increasing daily."—*The Milliner and Dressmaker.*

"Lay figures or models have been constructed in exact accordance with Hogarth's Line of Beauty. Ample space is secured for the play of the chest and lungs, thus at the same time preserving health, and improving the contour of the figure of the wearer."—*The Queen.*

Any Corsets not bearing this Trade Mark are not genuine, and only imitations.

Nor is this the only *tournure* that fashion has introduced. I do not know whether you will understand me, but it is now the fashion to be extremely *bombée*—and *bombée* every lady is. Those who are not so naturally resort to art, and I have seen an artificial bomb which I must recommend to your notice. It is of india-rubber and hollow, and perforated to allow the free circulation of air and perspiration. It is covered with fine white cambric, and is trimmed round with lace, so that even if seen by an indiscreet eye it looks merely like a pretty chemise concealing the real bomb. It is placed under the stays or over, *ad libitum*, and is so well made that even the lady herself who wears it may deceive herself if she will.

A little lace handkerchief, however, artfully thrust into the pockets of the stays, answers the same effect. But as I am bound to chronicle every novelty, so have I chronicled the new india-rubber. I have done.

*Advertisement and extract from Alice's Bible, The 'Journal des Modes', 1879.*

Thus, when she read in a copy of the new Croydon Advertiser, discovered on an adjacent seat in the almost empty horse omnibus which had carried her from Brixton that very morning, that Professor Faber from Vienna was demonstrating his Talking Machine at the Palais Royal, she made a mental note to investigate this new wonder at the earliest possible opportunity. It arrived sooner than expected. The cousin upon whom she hoped to call in Soho Square had departed, according to a neighbour, on a visit to a relative taken unexpectedly ill in Lancashire; the Palais Royal was only a step or two away, and it was a fine day.

Unfortunately, and one deviation always seems to pressage another, a notice on the great gilded door announced that Professor Faber was also regrettably indisposed.

"Another anthropoglossus, no doubt," announced a deeply resonant cultured baritone from somewhere above Alice's head.

"I beg your pardon!" She turned and looked up. Alice measured exactly five foot four inches, as she knew very well from the dressmaker's dummy in her spare room. She knew her other measurements accurately from the same source and although she would never have discussed them with a gentleman, she suddenly found herself making comparisons.

Six foot? He must be all of that, even six foot six. He was certainly dark, not bad looking either, and he wore black, black entirely. That was the impression Alice received from her lowly prospect of the centre of the gentleman's chest.

As he stepped back – he had been reading Professor Faber's announcement over her shoulder – perspective was restored. Black the gentleman wore, certainly, and his linen was respectably white, the cravat elegantly arranged. In his button-hole he wore a white rose, Alice was flummoxed between an instinctive desire to maintain the proprieties – no respectable lady spoke to a strange man, certainly not outside the Palais Royal in Argyll Street – and pure curiosity.

"Forgive me, sir," she said, with asperity. "Were you addressing me?" The man's manner, she thought, was extremely odd, and blinked, for his hat suddenly lifted itself in a waggish tilt before settling back on his head.

"I said, another anthropoglossus," explained the man. "That was to be another talking machine, claimed to have been made some years ago, just a fraudulent instrument for extracting investment from the pocket of an optimistic and foolish young peer. None will work, Ma'am, none at all, until my own investigations are completed."

Eyeing the hat apprehensively, wondering if perhaps the Journal des Modes were not uncomfortably near the mark in that anno domini was creeping up and she seeing things, Alice was incapable of walking away.

She felt rivetted to the spot. The man smiled, displaying an even set of white teeth.

"You are investigating talking machines, sir?"

"Indeed Ma'am", and the hat lifted once more. "Among many other things."

"Like this," he added, as the hat lifted yet again. "My patent hat-raiser, Ma'am."

He pulled a fine rubber tube from a pocket until an apparently endless length arrived finally at a curious bulb. He pressed it several times and the hat bobbled obligingly.

"Allow me to introduce myself," and he bowed. "Ferneley is the name, Professor Jabez Ferneley, your servant – humble ornament of the Faculty of Philosophy at the University of Augsberg. At your service, Ma'am."

During the exchange the tube had become entangled hopelessly with the Professor's eloquent right hand. With the left he now removed his hat, unclipped a tiny contrivance from under the brim and performed a series of flapping motions until he was free of the muddle. He threw it away and dabbed ineffectively at a sore area on his forehead. He reminded Alice of a sea lion which had performed at the Crystal Palace.

"That's better," he announced, restoring his headgear and then raising it in the conventional manner. "Not practical, ma'am. Gives you a headache. I'll invent a better one tomorrow." Suddenly he paused, seeming to notice Alice for the very first time.

"Madame," he exclaimed, as if a great light suddenly glowed over her head. "Madame! I knew it! Let me look at you!"

Alice stepped back in some alarm.

The Professor had once more removed his headgear.

"Madame, I am sure . . . it must be . . . your name, ma'am? You must certainly be Polish!"

"You make a mistake, sir," said Alice, breathlessly, not even certain if Poland was in Europe or Africa. "I am Mrs Burrows and I live in Brixton and . . ."

She was not allowed to finish. "Ah, but you see, ma'am. Matrimony has robbed you of the name I seek." Alice found herself at some pains to reply. The man's personality was compelling.

"I was born Alice Sorby, in Brixton, sir, although I fail entirely to comprehend how the matter should concern you." Alice had retrieved a little of her dignity; "and now, if you'll allow me to pass . . . I have better things to do than to stand here arguing with a complete stranger."

"Sorby, Sorby! You see, I was right! My fate is fulfilled. It is merely a linguistic corruption. Sobiecka! Don't you see? In me, dearest madame, you perceive the re-personification of no less a person than Prince Charles. You believe, of course, in transmigration? You, madame, you are my Polish Princess! Permit me, dear lady, to present a small token of my esteem."

Alice found herself clutching the white rose from the Professor's button-hole.

The persuasive chatter continued into Regent Street and the coffee house in Piccadilly to which her new surprising acquaintance led the way. In the confines of the high-sided stall his gesticulations were restricted but his enthusiasm diminished not at all. He sat next to her in the horse bus to Brixton. When she descended at Acre Lane beyond the railway bridge and draper's shop with the goat farm opposite, he had noted her address, and promised to call on her the following Wednesday. Alice hadn't been courted with such whirlwind enthusiasm since Charlie Burrows came into her life twenty-five years ago.

She had few illusions. She remembered Charlie with gratitude, for to the brief interlude with him she owed both her home and the adequate financial provision of a far-sighted insurance policy. In Charlie's day, insurance was not very remote from the primitive tontine, and the payment of premiums to provide against a breadwinner's decease was considered both a temptation of providence and an unnecessary extravagance.

Algernon Lambert was another case entirely. With him she had fallen hopelessly in love, regretting only that in the moral climate of the time her affaire must always remain clandestine. As she regularly polished the silver tea set which had been Algy's parting gift, together with the banker's order which arrived by messenger a few days after what turned out to be his complete disappearance, she thought sometimes of where he might be now. She often wondered at his strange choice of a token and how he had come by it, for it wasn't new. She had been so distracted on that final night long ago that she had scarcely taken in the significance of his wild rambling. There was talk of a ship called the Ke-Ying, new horizons, and wild threats. If he remained a moment longer, he had said several times, he would be hanged for strangling a certain Mrs Prendergast. He had been too distraught for her to take seriously his invitation to her to sell up, leave everything and throw in her lot with his new adventure.

Alice's courage had failed her and he had gone away. She knew of Melissa, but Mrs Prendergast was something of an enigma.

She was in the crowd acclaiming the opening of the Great Exhibition in the Crystal Palace in Hyde Park in 1851, and was intrigued to see an extravagantly robed Chinaman among the party of notables processing

*He—Sing in the Royal entourage at the opening of the Crystal Palace in Hyde Park, 1851, from a painting by Henry Selous.*

about the Queen and the Prince. He walked with a curious, rolling gait, taking steps to either side so that there was always a space in which he remained the centre of attraction. Someone near her in the crowd said this was the captain of that same Ke-Ying of which her lover had spoken and she had considered whether the Chinaman might be approached with an enquiry. Did he, she wondered, speak English? She couldn't come easily to him among the potentates and ambassadors. Even to a fellow-countryman the situation couldn't be easily explained. Alice had her pride. The hurt was almost healed. Algernon was best left a memory.

Life proceeded with turgid monotony. Gentlemen came and went in the life of Alice Burrows. So preoccupied had she become with the approach of middle age that she was surprised to find her pulse quickening at the thought of the coming Wednesday and the Professor's visit. He could very well be a rogue. In conversation she had discovered that he spoke no German, only a little French, and this was difficult to reconcile with his claim to an Augsberg degree; but at least he was different. Princess indeed! She put the white rose in a tiny vase marked 'A Present From Brighton".

The following morning she made certain investigations. Finding little of interest in a single volume encyclopaedia in her own book-case, she paid a visit to Mr Massey who kept a small bookshop near the Bon Marche and was an old friend. "Bonnie Prince Charlie? The Stuarts, Mrs Burrows? I've the very thing. No, you wouldn't have to buy it. Come into the back room and we'll see what we can find. Whatever leads you to such an . . . er . . . esoteric study?"

"Just something I read in a book," said Alice, surprised at her own embarrassment.

The Stuarts, she discovered, had travelled extensively. She found that the Pretender had indeed married Clementina Sobiecka. Henry, another member of the family, became a Cardinal. In small print in a very old volume she found a strange piece of what her mother used to call "gratuitous information" in a footnote. Many Stuarts, it seemed, suffered an odd malformation of the hands. They were born with twelve fingers, which was probably why the Professor made more of an impact than he might have done!

He arrived on the Wednesday in a hansom, punctual to the minute, bearing a large bunch of white roses, a folio of papers and a box. With a flamboyant gesture he took her hand, pressed it to his lips and suggested that it was a beautiful day to be visiting a Princess. Alice was going to protest that it looked like rain and he'd better come inside since the neighbours were becoming curious, when she was able to observe her visitor's hands. On each, beyond the little finger, a small vestigial digit hung loose. She wondered, with some apprehension, if this could indeed be the sixth finger of the Stuarts.

Try as she would, she couldn't persuade herself to adopt a legacy, even an imagined one, of Polish Royalty. Since both her father, who had been a clockmaker, and her mother, who had been in service, were born within the sound of Bow Bells, they were proud to be known as Cockneys, and Alice had never suffered any aspiration to nobility other than an almost forgotten, infantile desire to dress up as a Pearly Queen.

The white roses went into the big Doulton pottery vase in the window, resplendent against the be-tasselled and draped red plush curtains. The Professor waxed ecstatic. Only a Princess, he enthused, could make such an elegant arrangement. He wandered about the room admiring and commenting, finally coming to rest upon the horsehair sofa, where, for a moment, his eloquence foundered.

"You are in trade, Professor?" asked Alice tentatively.

"Trade, ma'am? Alas, a genius like mine must not allow itself to be constricted by the sordid shackles of commerce. My brain, ma'am, must work for the benefit of mankind. One day, perhaps, I shall achieve immortality!"

*Addiscombe Military Academy, training centre for the East India Company about 1850.*

"You mean with your talking machine?"

"Philosophy, dearest Clementina, if I may thus address you, is about to leap forward into vast new arenas. The talking machine certainly receives a degree of my attention. The mysteries of electricity are much more absorbing." He dropped his voice to a conspiratorial whisper, at which Alice's Pekinese, Ching, having busied himself on the fringe of the ceremonies of arrival and welcome, now fixed his beady eyes upon the visitor and growled. "Have you considered, Princess, the vast possibilities of Perpetual Motion?" Alice hadn't, considering privately that the world suffered already from an excess of activity. Why invent something else that never stayed still?

She listened for a long time. The Professor, it seemed, lived in Croydon, near the Addiscombe Academy where the East India Company Officers received their military training. He became reminiscent about the cadets, told of their expeditions to out-of-bounds areas, and how, when the Great Exhibition opened and they were not allowed to attend, a party donned full regimentals and marched all the way to Hyde Park where they enjoyed an official reception.

"I was there," said Alice, enthralled. "Did you see the Chinaman?", but the Professor was already off on a new tack, describing his home. Rose Cottage, he called it, and it lay on the boundary of the old Academy grounds near the railway bridge, which, of course, had long ago carried the road over the Canal. "They should have kept the Canal," he mused, "and when they couldn't keep that, they should have kept the atmospheric railway, but they've changed again. Steam trains now; can't make up their minds!"

If they would only pursue the Ferneley Perpetuator all the problems would be solved, but the Croydon Microscopal Club, which had once been interested, now was concerned only with microscopes – what could you expect with a surgeon in the Chair? Couldn't the Perpetuator be adapted for medical purposes? "Couldn't it?" Alice nodded, although she really didn't understand at all.

*Form of Certificate for Election of Members.*

—o—

**CROYDON MICROSCOPICAL CLUB.**

**Mr.**

**of**

**being desirous** of becoming **a** Member of this Club, we beg to **recommend** him for Election.

*(on my personal knowledge.)*

**This Certificate was read** 187

**The Ballot will take place** 187

—o—

**NOTE.—The foregoing Rules were adopted at a general meeting of the original members of the Club, held on the 16th of March, 1870, when the following gentlemen were elected as officers and members of the committee :—**

*President*—MR. HENRY LEE, F.L.S., F.G.S., F.R.M.S., &c.

*Treasurer*—MR. JOHN WICKHAM FLOWER, F.G.S., &c.

* *Hon. Sec.*—MR. HENRY LONG.

*Committee*

**MR. JOHN** BERNEY, F.R.M.S.; MR. WILLIAM REEVES COOPER; MR. **ALFRED** HAWARD; DR. HENRY LANCHESTER; DR. HENRY J. STRONG.

* **Communications** to be addressed to the Hon. Sec., 99, High Street, Croydon.

*An enrolment form for the Croydon Microscopal Club.*

His only sponsor, the Academy itself, had closed down nine years ago, and now the Engineer Instructor, who had continued to work with him on the project in the garden of Rose Cottage had to get himself killed by a train. They should have kept the canals. "Money, dear Clementina, not on my own account, you understand, is of the essence. I have all the drawings here."

Alice thought the time had arrived to change the subject, and suggested that a glass of claret would not come amiss. She pulled the ornate bell cord which hung down beside the fireplace.

She was beginning to wonder again. The claims to genius could be real, so might a conviction of Royal descent. There were, she knew, several claimants to blood relationship with the British Monarchy. Even a belief in re-personification might be genuine; but the three factors all at once were difficult to swallow, and now, was he going to ask for money? Pity he was so damnably attractive, and what could one make of the six fingers? She tugged the bell cord a second time.

Either the bell was shamed into silence by the presence of an inventive genius, or Lizzie, the adenoidal skivvy, was out in the garden reporting on proceedings to a colleague over the back fence. Alice descended to the basement scullery to investigate. She heard Ching growling as she prepared the tray. Ching, she thought, was jealous, he probably resented male intrusion into the household.

When she returned with the claret and some arrowroot biscuits, the Professor still sat on the sofa. On an occasional table beside him he had set up the contents of his box, a dimunitive model of what looked like three water wheels set in tandem. Wires dangled from it which, he said, must be joined to magnetic coils to provide the electric force to make the contrivance work – for ever. "Perpetual Motion, Princess! I'm afraid your little Ching is frightened of my apparatus!"

So that was why Ching had protested. Only much later when she went to make tea for her guest did she wonder yet again. The silver teapot on the sideboard faced right instead of left. She didn't think she'd made a mistake after the last cleaning session. Lizzie was not supposed to touch the ornaments and she was meticulous in their placing.

Jabez, as he insisted upon being called in public – and it was difficult to know how to address him – set himself out to be charming. In the afternoon they dined in the small room at the back of the house, and even the adolescently gauche Lizzie was so impressed by the handsome visitor that the whole meal was served without a hitch. The Professor expressed himself enchanted, and when, in the evening she accompanied him to the end of the road, Alice, impressed that he hadn't outstayed his welcome, had to admit that the day had been a pleasant one. It was good to have a man about the house once more. His new ideas broke the monotony, and he didn't speak of money again.

On three consecutive Wednesdays he returned. Each time he brought white roses. Each time he was clad in immaculate black. The neighbours speculated on a new romance, and on the third visit Alice suggested that the following week she should return the compliment. Appreciating the difficulties of bachelor housekeeping, she would arrange a lunch basket for three, and bringing Lizzie as her chaperone, pay a visit to Rose Cottage. She would hire a pony and trap from the stables by the goat farm.

They were taking their glass of claret in the drawing room when the companionable silence was shattered by a peremptory banging on the front door. Alice, wondering who could be so urgent in the middle of a September morning, didn't wait for Lizzie's routine. Her righteous indignation was disarmed by the appearance of a small, none-too-presentable urchin. Tears stained his features and he was out of breath. Alice recognised Tommy, the lad who made deliveries for the bookshop.

"Sorry, mum," he gabbled, panting. "It's Mister Massey, mum. 'E's bin took queer. Lyin' on the floor an' starin'. An' I bin to all the uvver places an' no-one'll come an' I know you're a friendav 'is so c'd you com'n 'elp. Only make it quick 'cos 'e'll die."

Alice didn't stop for her bonnet. She just called Lizzie to look after the Professor and followed the diminutive messenger.

Poor old Mr Massey had suffered a seizure. Alice, who knew everyone, sent the boy to the doctor with a note, but when he came there was little to be done. It took an hour or so to fetch in the books displayed on the outside shelves and to work out how to fit and bolt the shutters. It took a considerable time to compose a letter to Mr Massey's sister-in-law, who lived in Streatham. She handed it to Tommy, with a few coppers, telling him to come to Acre Lane for something to eat when the mission was done. Then she took the key from Mr Massey's pocket and locked up.

When she got home she was struck by the silence. Ching didn't come to the door. A distant scratching soon discovered him, shut in the tool shed. Lizzie reported that the Professor had waited an hour, taken another glass of claret and then said he ought to be going.

Alice sat in the silent drawing-room waiting for Tommy, who, she realised, might not return until the following day if there was any delay at the Massey Cottage. The chill of the September evening prompted her to lay another log on the fire. Poor Mr Massey, she would miss him, but it was good to go like that, suddenly, among the things one loved. He had loved his books, and now the widowed sister-in-law in Streatham, whom she knew as his only surviving relative, who was always in and out of the pawn shop, would perhaps be able to afford a few proper clothes for those boys of hers. Adam, the eldest, she had met and knew as a bright lad. He could be encouraged to take on the shop – or would it be better to sell off the stock? It wouldn't fetch much. The brother was a tearaway. Would he go to sea? That was what he said he wanted.

Pouring herself a glass of claret she happened to look at the sideboard. Something was different. The mind rejects the unpleasant, that which offends, what it doesn't want to know. The fact, nevertheless, remained. The Professor had gone . . . so had the silver tea service.

She didn't want to believe her eyes. Slowly she rose from her armchair, still not believing, but there was the space, and in it lay a piece of paper.

"Princess," she read, and she seemed to hear the resonant baritone echoing hollowly through the room. "I could not ask you again. Your Prince is desperate. Your silver is safe. I shall take it to Mr Tuson on Brixton Hill and leave the ticket with him. A thousand apologies and regrets. One day, God willing, I shall return. Charles."

On Thursday morning, Alice quickly walked the short half-mile to the establishment of Mr Henry Tuson, where the three brass balls hung at the top of the hill. Like most of his kind he was dealer as well as pawnbroker. She knew him well, for over the years he had sold her several pieces of jewellery. He sometimes sent a card when he thought he had found something she might like.

He looked up as she entered the shop. "Mr Tuson," she said, without preamble. "You have a teaset for me I believe."

"That's right, Mrs Burrows. Nice pieces, just your taste. There's one pound, two-and-six to pay."

Alice, with no comment, handed over a sovereign and half-a-crown. Was the Professor only a fool? He could have raised a lot more than that, even from Mr Tuson. For a whole week, involved as she became with Mr Massey's affairs, the matter rankled.

So, on the Wednesday she resolved to carry out her original plan. In a hired pony and trap, with Lizzie beside her and a lunch basket for three on the floor she set out for Croydon. Lizzie had to walk up the hill to spare the pony, but after the Telford crossing she sat beside her mistress. They passed the tram sheds on the left, and the stocks on the Green below Streatham's Church of St Leonard. They trotted past the Greyhound, where a short diversion permitted the exchange of compliments with an already rejuvenated Mrs Massey, and came to Hermitage Bridge over the Wandle at Norbury. At Thornton Heath Pond by Collyers Water Lane, haunt of the old charcoal burners, the pony was allowed refreshment at the

*Tuson's Corner, Brixton Hill. A pawnbroker commemorated by a street sign.*

*Thornton Heath Pond. On Alice's route to Addiscombe.*

trough. At Broad Green they reined to the left and Addiscombe.

Rose Cottage had been exactly as the Professor described it. It was near the site of the old Academy, and now new streets and houses were springing up all around it. It was just beyond the Railway Bridge, and when Alice, followed by Lizzie, sniffing violently in her agitation, laid a hand on the gate, upon which the word "Rose" was still barely decipherable, it fell off its hinges.

Down the overgrown path they went, lifting their skirts to avoid the brambles, briars and nettles. A few tired white roses were in evidence, and around the back a large structure which seemed to consist of three great disintegrating wheels loomed among the straggling weeds.

As they emerged once more into the lane an old man came through the hedge opposite. He seemed surprised to see them. He tipped his cap. "Lookin' for someone, Ma'am?"

"Yes," said Alice Burrows. "Does Professor Ferneley live hearabouts?"

A speculative look came into the old man's eye. He tested a gatepost, then leaned on it. "Let's see now, Ferneley, Ferneley. Would that be the inventor chap used to work up at the Military School?"

"That's right, a very tall, good looking gentleman. Do you know him?"

"I did know him alright, M'm, but 'e ain't been seen round these parts for nigh on ten year."

Alice gave him a coin and watched him amble away towards the main road.

What had Jabez said at their first meeting? Something about an anthropoglossus? She'd remembered because it was so strange. It had been a hoax to entice money from an optimistic and foolish young peer.

Alice had a rare sense of humour. She could laugh at herself, and did. "I'll wager it cost him more than twenty-two-and-six!"

"What's that, Mum?" asked Lizzie in some astonishment.

"Never mind, child," said Alice, in a quieter voice. – "Let's get home."

What had befallen her poor, six-fingered Pretender? He hadn't been a complete illusion like her temporary elevation to the Polish Nobility, which she had never believed in any case. With a sigh she mounted the step into the trap and pulled Lizzie up after her.

You didn't, she philosophised, as they trotted along the High Road, necessarily grow wiser with years – just more experienced.

And on the morrow there would be the bookshop – and Adam.

Adam was a bright lad. If she'd had a son of her own she'd have liked a boy like him.

# Fake Teapot

When Adam Massey came out into the evening sunshine of St James', he was thoughtful. He couldn't forget the comment about that Chinese artist. It kept coming back like a catchy tune. The old man from the museum, looking, wisely, thought Adam, for oriental paintings when most people considered them a drag on the market, said it was translated from an ancient Pekinese document. "So lifelike were his pictures that, when his time came to pass over, he just opened a doorway on one of his landscapes, passed through, and was never seen again." Chinese paintings? He decided to put some by for himself. They turned up quite frequently in job lots and they didn't take up much room. They were cheap. They could be rolled up and stacked in a corner.

Art was a matter of perception. Impression could strike the overall vision more sharply than miniscule definition. The Chinaman must have been a very great artist, but did anyone now know his name?

Such interludes lent spice to the daily monotony of dealing, if you could regard the handling of beautiful, precious things so prosaically. Fifty pounds wasn't bad for a pair of Bartolozzi prints, and as for those blue and white Chinese vases, well, they might have been Kien Lung, but who could be sure? They'd been too big and heavy to handle easily, and he hadn't had a chance to examine them when the American clamoured for a price. Heavens! Had they been Wan Li? He shrugged his shoulders. With such things and such people the only solution was to think of a number and double it. Newly rich Americans were inclined to buy on a whim. He might bring the vases back!

The American had counted out his hundred and twenty sovereigns with the loud-mouthed abandon of a successful Californian gold-prospector, and such careless extravagance deserved what it got. If we went on selling all our best pieces to South African and American millionaires there'd be nothing left for the real connoisseurs. No doubt about it, good things were hard to find. But dealers, surely, had always said that, and wasn't it the very reason why the best was rare and expensive?

Adam was a realist. One hundred and seventy pounds in a day. Time was, in the old bookshop in Brixton, when it would have represented more than a year's takings. For a moment, against the gleaming, dark green and varnished shopfront, with the shining brass-fitted door and the gold-leafed fascia, Adam saw once again the cardboard clutter of the old book-shop in Brixton as it was when "Aunt" Alice first took him there . . . how long ago was it? . . . thirty-five years. Time had flown. Berry Brothers with their exclusive vintages and Locke's the old-time hatters may have been in St James' longer, but "A. Massey, Works of Art" certainly looked smarter.

Mrs Burrows had proved more than a friend. When Tommy arrived with her message, on that Wednesday evening so long ago, knocking on the door of the ramshackle cottage below Streatham Common, Mrs Massey was far too preoccupied with the preparation of a stew made from scrag ends and leftover cabbage stalks, to pay attention to details of the death of her departed husband's brother. Only later did she weep hopelessly, and then not with a sense of loss, but in frustration at the apparently remorseless fate which in her present trouble could still plague her with more. She was not a practical woman. There was, meanwhile, nothing she could do. Tommy would have to wait until her son Adam came home, and goodness knew where he'd gone. He was never there when he was wanted. If he had stayed at her beck and call the family would have starved long since.

When Adam, then fourteen, but not looking his years, finally did arrive, it was already late and he was tired, hungry and cold. He found Tommy huddled fast asleep by the front door and only after hearing the garbled relation of his uncle's death several times did he realise that here, out of the blue, might be a way of relieving his family's poverty-stricken plight. He gave his mother the few pence he had gathered minding horses for the gentry at Norbury Races and arranged for Tommy to stay by the meagre fire for the night.

Early the following morning, in tattered, ill-fitting clothes, and without his worn boots, which, his mother insisted, from force of habit, must be kept for special occasions, he trudged to Brixton with Tommy.

Adam smiled to himself at the recollection of the breakfast Alice had provided. That had been her forte. She had a perfect sense of priority. Breakfast first, and they had gorged on fresh bread and butter and eggs and bacon. Never was banquet so delicious. Lizzie had been fully instructed.

Then Alice herself, returned from Brixton Hill, had got busy with pencil, paper and tape-measure, and having shown the boys the bathroom, a new mystery, and filled the to-them vast mahogany cased tub with hot water, told them to "clean up" and "wash behind their ears, mind." Then she had vanished.

She returned within the hour loaded down with several large parcels bearing the name of the large outfitters by the railway, directed the boys to a spare room and told them to "get dressed".

By this time Adam and Tommy were feeling almost naked in their new-found cleanliness and they were worried by the pervading smell of carbolic. But they did their best, scarcely recognizing the images Alice insisted on showing them in a wardrobe mirror.

Only then, feeling as if everyone was looking at him in his new clothes, was Adam taken to see his Uncle's shop. At his request Tommy came too and he hadn't left the Massey menage since.

In the back room of the shop, behind the old chenil-covered armchair with the horsehair spilling out of it in which the book dealer had daily dozed and spent so many of his leisure hours, Adam found his uncle's savings. Alice opened the iron box with one of the keys she had taken from the dead man's waistcoat. It was full of coin, some gold. Perhaps because he dealt in so much of it Mr Massey had never trusted paper.

Adam stood in the musty volume-laden room and smiled at his "Aunt". Then, telling her he'd be back on the morrow, he helped replace the shutters and, walking awkwardly in his new boots, set off to give his mother the good news. Under his arm he carried the heavy iron box.

Two sovereigns only he kept back for his capital, and as soon as Uncle Arthur was buried – Alice paid for the funeral – he restarted the business on his own account.

He sold books for a farthing if they looked at all respectable; if they had pictures he sometimes got a penny. The rag a' bone man had obviously been one of Uncle Arthur's main suppliers, and from him there was sometimes a barrow-load to be bought for sixpence. Adam began to read, learned the names of authors, and soon came to realise that some of the better-dressed callers who came from farther afield than Brixton, were looking for certain things. Books with coloured prints in them were wanted, books on hunting and travel; musty, tooled leather bindings with latin texts, with pictures of birds, flowers and fishes. While he sold much of what he bought to make a living, some of the more likely volumes, similar to those which sold very quickly, he stacked in the back room where his uncle had once sat talking to his friends. He spent a whole Sunday, in spite of his mother's protests, greasing and painting the old, broken down barrow which stood rotting in the lean-to in the tiny yard behind the shop.

Alice became very interested in the bookshop. Sometimes she bought for herself, sometimes suggested that a volume might be marked up at a higher price, and she helped Adam clear away most of the long-standing junk. He put up more shelves in the cleared spaces.

One day Adam took his barrow to a clergyman's house in Sydenham, and having piled it high for a shilling he was asked by a parlourmaid to come round to the kitchen. The Lady of the House, she said, wanted to see him. Adam was seventeen, and the barefoot ragamuffin from Streatham was now respectably clad in a dark worsted suit bought in the market in Electric Avenue. He wore a stiff collar which he changed each week, and his tie was neat. His shoes were blacked and he sported a curly-brimmed bowler. The vicar's widow was not as formidable as he feared.

"Do you only buy books, Mr Massey?"

Conscious that he might have to rely on casual book sales to feed himself for the rest of the week, Adam paid out all he had in his pockets, two sovereigns and a crown, for a silver coffee pot, a Chelsea vase – at least, that was what the vicar's widow told him it was and he was in no case to argue – and a finely carved mahogany elbow chair. He tied the chair to the barrow, on top of the books, and put the two other pieces in a sack slung between the handles.

The heavy load nearly broke away under its own weight on the slippery cobbles of Knight's Hill, which, placed there to assist the passage of horses going up, did little to help a book dealer coming down, and Adam resolved to improve matters by buying himself a horse.

Alice, who liked silver, gave him three sovereigns for the coffee pot and stood it on the sideboard with her tea service. Having recently spent an interesting morning watching the disposal of a "Gentleman's Effects" in Christie's Great Auction Rooms, in Pall Mall, she suggested that the chair and the vase might fetch a good price there. Meanwhile Adam had heard about the book auctions at Sotheby Wilkinson and Hodge, off the Strand.

One Monday morning, having spent a restless weekend, worrying lest his temerity be scorned, Adam screwed up his courage and donned his best suit. He had two by then, and he added a pair of lavender spats to set off a new bowler hat. A friendly carter, – what had his name been? Bert, that was it, agreed, for a minimal fee of sixpence, to provide wheels for the expedition. He would have used the barrow, but Alice said he had to learn to make an impression. To do that appearance was important. Pushing a barrow in spats, well, it just didn't look right.

He'd had qualms as they loaded up those books, sixpence that he could ill afford, down the drain? The sun had shone, but as they clattered through the traffic, Adam had an unreasoning foreboding that it might rain and ruin the stock. Bert, who couldn't even read, insisted that it didn't need covering.

The clerk at Sotheby's, where the books were unloaded, sniffed and eyed Adam without enthusiasm. He had a dewdrop on his nose. "They honestly come by, Mister?" Adam bridled, and it was Bert who stopped him re-stacking the whole lot back on the cart and returning to Brixton. Seeing his reaction the clerk had softened a little. "We don't like things that are nikked, see. Suppose you'd have had a job to pinch that lot." And there had been a lot, Adam recalled. He wished he still had some of them today.

The reception at Christie's, more frosty perhaps, but less daunting, for at that time, while he had every intention of advancing his fortunes, Adam had no illusions about being a gentleman, provided hope. Some attention was paid to his chair, and then it was compared with a picture in a book, of which care was taken to conceal from him the title. Adam smiled wryly to himself. Chippendale's Directory. Well, you had to start learning somewhere. There'd been a console table and a pair of gilt mirrors in addition to the Chelsea vase, and all were received with favourable comment. Adam felt more optimistic.

His spirits soared three weeks later when the postman delivered two envelopes by two separate deliveries on the same day. He opened them with trembling fingers.

Next day a travelling sign-writer, a gipsy who painted caravans, took careful instruction. Adam Massey, Antiquarian bookseller and Antique Dealer, was in business. He opened his first banking account with two cheques from famous auction houses and a guarantee from Alice Burrows. His credit stood at eighty-two pounds. He bought a dappled pony with his first cheque and a second-hand delivery cart which he painted dark green and lined with yellow with the sovereigns he had for the coffee pot. Thereafter he was able to cast his net much wider, north to Chelsea, south to Croydon, and into the burgeoning suburbs east and west. He looked for more chairs and tables, for the furniture to go with them, for the odd piece of china, even glass. He looked at paintings, wondered about them, watched how his clients examined them, searched in his books for the names of artists. He built an outhouse behind the shop to display his new purchases, and London dealers began to call.

Meanwhile, with spare pence in his pocket, he had practically rebuilt the cottage in Streatham. His young brother, James, now fifteen, went to sea as a cabin boy. A distant cousin came to live with his mother. Alice, seeking a new distraction, and fascinated by the rising fortunes of her young protegé, suggested that he move to the house in Acre Lane, where, for some time he had been putting up for the night when he either worked late or had to be abroad early. There, in the Autumn of 1873, in spite of a rumble

*A modern sale at Sotheby King & Chasemore*

of protest from the ageing Ching, he took up his abode in two large rooms on the third floor.

Adam, lost in his daydream, there on the pavement in St James', suddenly realised that a dapper, rather portly gentleman in a grey tail-coat and top-hat, was speaking to him and looking concerned. "Are you unwell, Mr Massey."

"No, no, I'm quite alright, thank you Mr Duveen. Carried away by my thoughts, that's all. Were you able to purchase the Raffael?" Adam had been waiting for Duveen to enquire about a painting of his own, one he had almost forgotten from his book dealing days. When he moved shop, he had taken it home, and it had dropped behind a chest. It came from a long-established family, was certainly old, and cried out for expert examination, but now was not the moment.

A few pleasantries, and the famous art dealer passed on his way.

*St. James's Street where Adam Massey opened a shop and met Duveen.*

Rumour had it that his finances were not quite what they should be, but Adam liked the man. He had courage, and Adam remembered the day when he'd had little more than that to play with, himself. No dealer was worth his salt who wouldn't back his judgement with his last penny – and a little more. He passed into the mews, where his hack, another dapple, waited in the stable to take him home.

Tommy, who seemed to have been part of the scenery for years, had left the old mare saddled. The tack was immaculate; brass shone, her coat gleamed and hooves had been freshly oiled. Tommy had looked after the firm's animals ever since the first Brixton pony, but now he was worried, with many of his colleagues, that his employer might be thinking of deserting the custom of ages and taking to the internal – infernal some called it – combustion engine.

Adam tightened the girth, mounted, and rode down towards the Palace; a gentle canter along Pall Mall, and a wait for the traffic flow at Haymarket, where one of the new motor cars had broken down. Tommy shouldn't be so concerned. A commotion in Trafalgar Square announced yet another protest – was this one political? – there seemed to be disturbance of some kind every other day now – and he turned quickly into Whitehall, down toward Parliament Square and on over Lambeth Bridge. As he approached Kennington a peated section of the road warned of sickness or death in one of the adjacent houses. The sudden break in the rythmic beat of hooves again released the flood of memory.

He would be home in fifteen minutes, back in Acre Lane. There would be a welcoming fire, a meal fit for a king, and a glass of the good claret he'd put down, ten years since, with Alice's shrewd advice. She, alas, was no longer there to partake of it. In the same year that had seen the end of the old Queen's long reign, Alice Burrows, quietly and without any fuss, still talking about an exhibition at the Crystal Palace, had excused herself from the dinner table, saying she would return shortly. Lizzie had gone to investigate her non-reappearance. The old lady, happy and active to the last, had just fallen asleep in a big chair in the hall. Adam thought she would have liked that description of the death of the Chinese artist. She left him everything, even the silver teaset.

Lizzie? Adam smiled secretly to himself as he passed "The White Horse". A coach with a party of Cockney day trippers pulled noisily away, leaving in its wake two vociferous potmen, a pair of grooms, and the waving figure of the blowsy attendant of the whelk stall. " 'Bye 'bye, ducks!" "See yer Sat'dy, Bert!"

Yes, Lizzie's reaction to his move to Acre Lane had surprised everybody.

Her adenoids suddenly vanished. Alice, who had been on the point of finding another maid because the girl seemed to be losing interest in everything and breaking all the best china, was surprised when she appeared smart and smiling at the breakfast table, and was to be heard singing about her chores. For a long time Adam was unaware that anything had changed. Alice was perturbed, not so much because she laboured under any prudish illusions, but more because the boy didn't seem to notice. Not for three long years was Adam able to drag himself away from the ever-increasing demands of his business. He rose early, came home late. He visited faraway sales, went to museums, studied, but one night, just after his twenty-first birthday, having travelled all day on a train from Preston, he let himself in with his key at midnight. A tray with a plate of sandwiches and a bottle of stout were laid out on a table by the big armchair in front of the lowering fire when he lit the oil lamp. Normally when he returned late like this he would eat his food and creep up to his room without waking the household. No-one usually waited up, but tonight he was startled when a slight figure in cap and apron stirred in the chair normally occupied by Alice.

"Lizzie!"

Adam had never been a talkative man, but he thought a great deal. All afternoon, as the train rattled through the dull, drizzle-laden murk of industrial England, he had been conscious of an unaccustomed inner turmoil. There had been a young woman standing on the station at Crewe. She looked trim and smart. She was dark, and if not a beauty, at least attractive. She made Adam, in the crowded carriage, conversing with a bearded gentleman behind the gold Albert thick enough to anchor a battleship – industrial Midlanders were not coy about prosperity – feel isolated. As the train pulled away and the whistling, pulsating smoke engulfed her the girl turned round, and Adam found himself wishing that she was . . . Lizzie.

In the growler which carried him through the night to Acre Lane his feelings had polarized. For years his path had been smoothed. Last night in the Preston Hotel the food was bad, the waiter insolent. He had asked for a paper in the morning and they had brought the wrong one. They had mixed his shoes with those of a commercial traveller in the room next door, and the whole place was dirty.

In Brixton everything was spotless. His linen was always laid out – even his shoes were always cleaned. His sheets were comfortably smoothed with a glass stick. There was a smile with his morning tea and his freshly ironed newspaper, and that smile, which had become part of his life without his even noticing, always belonged to the same person.

So now he stood up and with his boot turned over the log in the grate. With his back to it he looked down at the small, appealing figure in the plush chair. He held out his hand. "I've been blind, too busy to notice. I've been thinking in the train all day. I think I'm in love with you, Lizzie. Will you marry me?"

"I've loved you ever since the day you came, Adam. But how can you love me? I've watched you. You like beautiful things. You gloat over some of those paintings of yours. I'm no beauty – you'll want a beautiful woman for a wife, not a plain little thing like me."

Adam looked at Lizzie in the candlelight.

"Bless you, Liz. Beauty is a personal thing. The worst rubbish can be tricked out to look pretty. It's what's inside that matters – personality, kindness, goodness generally. Beauty? To me you're lovely, and I want no-one else. Will you marry me?"

Next morning Alice deliberately refrained from comment when Adam, slightly red in the face, arrived a little late for breakfast, self-consciously adjusting his tie. Early activity in the household that day appeared to have started up on the third floor rather than in the basement. Liking to have things about her tidy Alice breathed a sigh of relief and set about arranging in her mind, a new regime in which she would become virtually a tenant in her own house. But she would know the landlord, and he was of her own choosing.

The shop was closed for two weeks during the honeymoon in Margate. Lizzie proved to have unsuspected depths. She was understanding, and she had a sense of humour.

"Are we always going to stay in Brixton, Adam?"

"Whatever makes you ask, Lizzie?"

"I meant not 'us', but the shop. Haven't you ever thought of where your best customers come from? I don't believe I've seen a single buyer who comes from Brixton, and you haven't spoken of any either. Ever thought of moving up to London yourself? You could do it, you know. There're better prices to be had up there."

"The overheads'd be higher too. Rents are expensive in London, and I wouldn't be able to get home so quickly." Adam kissed Lizzie and smiled. "If you think it's a good idea, Liz, I'll think about it. You've been lucky for me so far."

The young couple returned to Brixton and a new menage. Alice had moved into Adam's rooms and installed both a parlour and a kitchen maid. She awaited the arrival of a new cook. The newly organised household flourished. The business went from strength to strength.

The London establishment remained no more than an ambition for a long time. Alice was for rebuilding the Brixton premises and increasing the turnover there. She had a rosy dream of Lizzie as mother of a large family to which she could play grandmother. If that delightful circumstance could be realised, the thought of what she might regard as her own family, based on the house in Acre Lane and the shop in the High Road, would go a long way to compensate for what she regarded as the deprivations of her younger days. She could even enjoy being a matron.

But it was not to be. The years passed and a whole generation grew up about them, but Adam and Lizzie remained childless. The two women spent a great deal of their time at the Shaftesbury Home in Kennington, expending their maternal energies upon the welfare of some of the thousands of juvenile unfortunates clinging to a precarious survival in and around London.

Alice advanced gracefully in years. At sixty-five she still kept a lively interest in Adam's activities, still had a season ticket for the Crystal Palace. Lizzie, trim and neat at thirty-nine, was her constant companion. The two women were reconciled to Adam's removal recently to the West End where he had at last succeeded in obtaining the premises in St James'. For months he had detoured on his way to the auctions, planning in his mind what he would do when the elderly proprietor retired.

He had been there nearly a year when Lizzie, who now, since Adam was away most of the day, spent even more time at the Shaftesbury Home, discovered an addition to the Massey household.

He appeared in the heavy escorting grasp of an enlightened police constable who had no wish to burden his festive conscience with the arrest of a colourful juvenile three days before Christmas in the year 1895. He was hungry, found loitering by the bakery oven in a market side street, as he vehemently proclaimed, " 'Cos it was bloody cold!" He had a small, bright and intelligent face, announcing that he thought that he was "full ten year old" with a fine tattered arrogance.

His dress set him apart. No boots had he, and his torn jersey and ill-fitting breeches were unremarkable, but he had made an effort to improve his lot on his own account. He wore a coat, a coat he had made himself.

It was ill-stitched and odd, created from a hodge-podge of cast-off trifles, of bits and pieces of every colour and texture. It caught up here and drooped there, gaped in a few places, yawned in others, but it was undoubtedly a remarkable achievement for a starving street urchin. It was a coat of many colours. The owner of such a garment could only be called Joseph.

Lizzie took Joseph home for Christmas. He was scrubbed outside the scullery with Tommy's sardonic but willing assistance, and after Christmas he remained to help in the stable and the garden.

He had to go to school, of course, and to everyone's surprise he persevered with his lessons. When he was fifteen Adam took him to London and put him in the workshop. He became the general handyman. If a door stuck or a lock had to be picked one sent for Joseph. He became almost an institution.

Pure chance brought him one day into Adam's office with a small table which had just been repolished at a time when everyone except the manager had gone to lunch.

Joseph had lost his early, hunted look. He was part of the establishment. He liked antique furniture and could make an antique drawer which would pass for genuine. He could carve a piecrust top or a Chippendale ball-and-claw, and in his spare time he was making one of those miniature spiral staircases once favoured by the eighteenth century architectural carpenter apprentices. The only thing he had not yet tried was selling.

A cart piled high with furniture drew up. "Watch the shop, Joe!" called the manager, going outside. "I shan't be a moment."

The cart bore a controversial oak table which had to be lifted down for examination. The moment became five, and unnoticed except by Joseph, Hiram P. Wendell chose that moment to visit Adam Massey's establishment for the first time.

Hiram was large, loud and surprising. He wore a grey, dog-tooth check

*The Shaftesbury Home, Kennington, now the Church of England Children's Society.*

tail suit, a grey topper and a yellow waistcoat with gold buttons. His boots were in two-tone fine brown leather and his flamboyant stock was caught up with a very large diamond. He carried a heavy, gold-mounted stick.

Joseph saw his opportunity. Now he would make a sale. He wasn't the first to assume that here, at last, was Mr Money-Bags himself. Curbing the natural exuberance which almost spilled into a Cockney comment on the weather, he advanced with stiff and unaccustomed dignity.

"Good day, Sir. May I be of h'assistance?"

"Uh-huh."

"Wot was ye wantin'? – furniture, china?"

"Ah guess this ain't the proper sho-op fer what Ah'm wantin'," said Hiram, as Joseph, fearful lest his quarry escape, edged round between him and the door.

"How 'bout a fine Chippendale chair, now?" he said, seizing upon the piece nearest to hand. He'd repaired one of the front legs on that chair; interesting to see if the American noticed – Adam had been critical. That was the trouble with the Guv'nor, good feller no doubt, but everything had to be "just so".

"No, Ah guess not. Ah was lookin' fer a piece of silver; it's fer a friend back in the States, a Congressman, – you'd call him a Member of Parliament – Ah owe him a favour, but Ah don't think you'd have the right thing. He only collects one maker . . . a woman's name . . . now what was it?

Hester somethin' or other."

"Bateman, sir," said Joseph with a flourish. They all knew about Hester Bateman. The only silver in the place – Adam was not over-fond of metal – was a tea service which sat, useless, on the central top shelf of the bookcase in the office. It had been there since old Mrs Burrows died. The Guv'nor had said not to put it on display but that it was interesting because it had been made by a woman silversmith. Joseph had offered to clean it once and had been told to get on with something else so he assumed it wasn't important. Now he had a buyer for it.

"If you'd just sit down and wait 'ere, sir. I think there's somethin' in the office that's just right."

Outside, as Joseph could see through the window, a deal was in progress. The oak refectory table stood on the pavement, the passers-by dividing, as with variously peeved, haughty or merely interested expressions, they moved to either side of it. Joseph knew he should have called the manager, but this was a chance too good to miss. He would prove his worth.

He opened the bookcase and lifted out the tea set. He gave it a hurried rub on his green baize apron, placed it on a Sheraton tray and carried it into the shop.

"There y'are, sir. The finest bit o' 'Ester Bateman you'll find in a month o' Sundays. Just needs a bit of a polish to make it good as new. Is that wot you wus wantin'?"

"Gee, ah guess so," said Hiram, taken aback by the unexpected success of his enquiry. "How much."

Now Joseph was flummoxed. There was a silver tea service in a shop in Piccadilly for forty pounds and they all said, the dealers, that is, that it was much too dear. The Boss had said that he wouldn't give twenty for it. Perhaps silver tea services were just unsaleable when there was so much good porcelain to be had. He knew he mustn't hesitate.

"Well. It's rare, that is. Guv'nor was keepin' it fer a speshal client. Two 'undred an' fifty do yer?"

"That's steep," said Hiram, "but there doesn't seem to be much of this Hester Bateman stuff around. It's what they said to get. Two hundred and Ah'll take it."

Hiram paid with four fifty-pound notes. Joseph made a parcel, and by the time he had finished, the table was being carried into the mews, so no-one saw Hiram Wendell depart.

Joseph kept his sale secret until Adam returned from Cornwall three days later.

When, like a magician bringing a rabbit out of a hat, he gave Adam the money, he discovered that selling was not always as rewarding as he'd thought.

Adam took the money, blanched, started to say something, and bit his words.

Then he spoke very carefully. "Joseph", he said, "that was a good price, far more than it was worth, and I know you thought you were doing the right things, doing me a favour, in fact. Here's a sovereign. I realise you thought you were acting in my best interest, but let me tell you something you may find difficult to understand. Certain things are worth more than money. So, don't ever again, ever, understand, sell anything out of this shop unless I give you permission."

Joseph's only effort as a salesman upset Lizzie. She blamed Adam first, although it had been she who suggested taking the service to London for safe-keeping. "Couldn't you write to this American and cancel the sale? It was Aunt Alice's most precious thing, Adam. It really is too bad of Jospeh. And as for leaving it about for anyone to come and take . . . why couldn't you put it in the safe?"

"Lizzie, love, sentimental souvenirs don't go in the safe. We need that for valuables; there's nothing I can do. Joseph just took the money, he didn't take the man's address. We don't even know his name", and there, for more than six months, the matter rested. No-one mentioned the tea service, but the very avoidance of it in conversation set up a kind of unspoken friction. Even Joseph became sullen.

Then the miracle occurred.

Adam was sitting in his office. He disliked correspondence and left most of the letters for his manager's attention, but he had to sign the cheques. He looked up as the spring bell over the door clattered. Two men had entered the shop. One was tall and flamboyant and carried a parcel under his arm. The other was small, round, bespectacled and self-effacing. No doubt about it, they were Americans.

Adam advanced.

"Good morning, gentlemen."

"Mr Massey?"

"In person," said Adam. "What can I do for you?"

"Well now", began the tall man, "mah name's Hiram P. Wendell, President of Consolidated Mines back in the United States, an' there's a little matter Ah'd like to clarify – if that's the word. This, by the way, is Mr Fishwick; he's goin' to be coorator of a museum Ah'm settin' up in mah home town in California. Could we talk in your office?"

"Come this way, gentlemen," said Adam, wondering what Trans-atlantic marvel was about to be revealed.

The visitors arranged themselves in the two mahogany armchairs before Adam's desk, Hiram Wendell still hugging his parcel. The dealer waited.

"It's the silver service Ah bought when Ah was over in Febrooary," said Wendel. "Fishwick here says it couldn't possibly have been made by that Hester woman becaws it's the wrong shape, an' Ah'm hopin' we can come to some – er – accommodation for you to take it back. We could do an exchange or somethin'. Things in mah museum have got to be gen-u-ine. You see, Ah, personally don' know much about these things an' your man said . . ."

Adam put up a hand. "My dear sir," he said, with a sudden lightening of spirit. Normally his instinct would have been to argue until he was blue in the face rather than give best to a monied upstart like Wendell. But here, presented on a plate, was the solution to a problem which had plagued him for months. He'd asked everyone he knew in the Trade, even enquired at the auction houses. Wendell had remained an enigma. Suddenly, like a visiting angel, here he was, large as life, sitting in his office. Still, he couldn't accept, unquestioned, the opinion of an unknown from America like Fishwick.

"You know a lot about silver, Mr Fishwick?" Mr Fishwick had the grace to blush.

"It's not my speciality, Mr Massey, but you'll admit, I think, that the shape of that pot is not characteristic? I've looked up all the references and I can't find any cast finials like that. They should be turned. I admit that the marks look genuine, and the date letter for 1784, but wouldn't that be a little late for Hester Bateman? I looked her up too; she must have been born in 1711."

Adam had never followed that reasoning. A female silversmith at the age of 73? It was just possible. The family would, in any case, have used her mark while she lived. Whatever Fishwick said, he didn't believe the service could be a fake, but he was glad to refund the two hundred pounds. He explained the circumstances of the sale and Wendell congratulated him on the eagerness of his staff. "Wish Ah'd a few like that workin' fer me!" In a flush of good will, Adam invited the two visitors to dinner later in the week. It was over dinner that Fishwick came into his own.

Lizzie had the gift of putting a visitor at his ease and the recovery of the teaset had set her in a happy humour. She kept a good cook and the meal was well served. The wines were still in the Alice Burrows tradition. Wendell held forth monotonously about his museum, but Fishwick positively shone.

He spoke with authority about Italian classical paintings, waxed eloquent on Raffael and da Vinci, admired Rembrandt and Breughel; he spoke of a forthcoming visit to Ghent where he hoped to gather material for a thesis on the Van Eyck altarpiece.

Adam began to regret any hard feelings he had entertained about Fishwick. The man knew his pictures. He excused himself when the port had been poured and fetched the small panel from the spare room where it had lain ever since he had rescued it from behind the chest. A wave of nostalgia came upon him as he picked it up and wiped away the dust. It was a long time since he'd bought it – he'd still had the old green cart in those days; he wondered if a fantasy was about to be dispelled, a dream broken.

He knew the picture was old. It was almost black, and through the murk of centuries the outline of a nude figure could be faintly seen. The thick varnish would have to be removed before a proper examination, but a real picture man could assess the possibilities.

"What do you think of it, Mr Fishwick?"

It was a small panel, some eighteen by nine inches. Fishwick carried it under the gasolier, where the light was brightest. He turned it over, brought out a jeweller's glass from his pocket, and peered across the surface. "Is it for sale?"

"I'd never thought about it to tell the truth. I've had it for ysars. What do you think of it?"

"Wa-all. It's just strange we should be talking about Van Eyck. This can't be far off the period; must be from the early sixteenth century at least. If you look into the composition of the figure you could relate it to the Eve in Ghent Cathedral, but others did that subject too. It's too black. I can't see. All I can be sure of is that the period's possible."

"Cummon, Fishwick," interrupted Wendell. "That's the trouble with you professor types. Can't make up your minds. Ah wouldn't be a millionaire if Ah'd spent all mah time dancin' round the maypole. Know what? When Ah staked out mah claim Ah jus' didn't know if Ah'd be diggin' up plain dirt or gold dust. Ah'd a hunch on that claim an' Ah won. Ah've a hunch on this picture. What about it, Fishwick?"

Wendell had dined well. The curator refused to commit himself.

"Aw gee. Would you listen to all that? You say it's old. Pardon me, ma'am, for being so blunt. It's the way we do business in California. Lookee here, Adam, if ye'll excuse the familiarity – you don't use first names here like we do – Ah'll buy the panel here and now for five thousand bucks, outright, or Ah'll lay down two thousand and pay you half the balance of what Fishwick thinks it's worth after he's done his investigations."

"What d'you think, Lizzie? Can't you see how he talked the teaset out of

*The Titantic at point of impact from a watercolour by F.J.H. Gardiner.*

Joseph?" Lizzie just nodded.

"To use your own idiom, okay Hiram. I'll take the two thousand. If there's more to come I'll bring Liz over to the States to spend it. You can show me your museum and we'll have a nice long holiday." A convivial evening passed. There were smiles all round, even, next day, from Joseph.

The cable arrived unexpectedly after the incident had almost faded from Adam's mind. It was very much to the point.

"MASSEY ST JAMES LONDON
VAN EYCK ESTABLISHED DUVEEN VALUATION TWENTY THOUSAND DOLLARS YOUR REMAINING SHARE NINE THOUSAND CUMMONOVER WENDELL"

Adam sat at his desk with a vacant grin on his face. He and Liz were past fifty and they hadn't had a long holiday since Margate.

Presently he rose from his desk, took down his top hat, and pulled his gold-mounted stick from the stand. He walked along Pall Mall to the shipping office, observing as he went that there were now almost as many motor cars as horses. He remembered a night long ago, in Brixton, a cab journey very late, a whelk stall and loud, cheerful voices; then he thought of Lizzie, warmly young before a blazing fire, warm and responsive later in his arms.

The clerk behind the counter, who had handled much of Mr Massey's shipping, was very attentive. He made many suggestions. Adam allowed himself to be talked into a stateroom. Lizzie would like that.

A passage was at length booked on the maiden voyage of the new Atlantic leviathan. This was to be a holiday to end all holidays.

The ship was called the "Titanic."

* * *

A year later the shutters were up in Acre Lane and St James'. Adam had left a comprehensive will. Alice had taught him, among many things, to be methodical.

Tommy had his cottage and a pension, the maids and staff all had a lump sum, and Joseph had enough to set up in business as a restorer.

Captain James Massey, Adam's brother, was in Australia when he heard the news. His house in Melbourne had become a burden since the death of his wife five years ago. He had no children. The settlement of Adam's affairs required his presence in England. After selling up he found that he had far more money than he needed and he was already tired of roaming the world. He was fifty-two years old.

During a recent voyage he had carried a passenger, a Mr Foster who had a house called "Raymead" in Hertfordshire. Over a companionable drink one evening, exchanging shipboard confidences, he had said he'd like to be able to travel more and would, if he could find a reliable person to leave in charge of the estate.

When he came to London, Captain Massey telephoned him.

# Territorial Teapot

". . . and when he got to them, up there on the field, they were made of cardboard. All those tanks, you see, just cardboard stuck on bits of wood. This chap in my office saw them himself. It's all bluff, I reckon. This'll be over in a week or so, just as soon as Hitler sees we mean business."

"Don't be too sure, Corp. They said things like that about the last one."

Lance Corporal Ashley and the C.O.'s batman sat in the front seat of the bus as it rumbled along the Aylesbury Road. Indicated destination was Peckham Rye, but then the one behind said Croydon and the one behind that, Charing Cross. Yet all three proceeded in the same direction, along the same roads which had never formed part of the General Omnibus Company's network. At bridges the convoy stopped while unprospected heights were calculated. At one, tyre pressures had to be reduced to make clearance.

They were at their destination, on the threshold of the future. Three drivers stood importantly in the road. They, after all, for the moment directed the fate of the company. The N.C.O.s stood separately, and one or two of the more venturesome of the khaki-clad passengers had descended too. They looked up and down the road in a limbo of uncertainty waiting for orders.

The notice board assumed the existence of a Sports Club. The name had been painted out in the latest security drive. The Corporal recognised it. "That's Huxley," he said, and the name echoed sibilantly along the stragglers. "Huxley," they said. "Huxley, Huxley? That's in Hertfordshire."

The place had been the social centre provided by an enlightened paper manufacturer for his staff. It still kept the title of Huxley House, but the last Huxley had been dead for ten years, only memory of a patriotic, colonially-minded family which, after a glorious Victorian renaissance of considerable political and financial achievement, barely weathered the holocaust of 1914–18. The younger Huxleys perished in it in various degrees of ineffectual glory. The older members of the family contrived, in the increasingly unfavourable social climate of the period, to keep the homefires burning with diminishing warmth and grandeur until the late twenties. Then the only remaining ember of a fire kindled shortly after the arrival of Conquering William, finally flickered weakly and went out. Distant relatives were located with difficulty, six of them widely scattered round the world. There was enough money to make them all unexpectedly rich. None wanted to be tramelled with a large, cumbersome estate, but one was acquainted with Wilkinson, manufacturer of distinguished note-papers. Wilkinson was making a great deal of money. He bought Huxley House for a song. It was a good investment. People came to work for him for the sake of the sports and social facilities.

In the late summer of the year 1939, when the convoy of commandeered red buses attempted to leave the road which had been there since Roman times, the occupants, in self-conscious khaki, had to perform a duty for which their weekend training as Searchlight Engineers, 30th Batt. (London Electrical) to be exact, had provided no instruction. One of the gateposts outside the old lodge which now dispensed confectionery, had to come down to allow the column to enter. The Territorial volunteers in the leading vehicle made their first contacts with the Hertfordshire natives there. By dint mainly of enthusiasm the post was very quickly, if not efficiently, removed. One of the batmen, a married man of thirty-five with children surprised himself with the success of his gauche effrontry and made an assignment, under the noses of her parents, with the twenty year old daughter of the house. The convoy eventually moved incongruously up the half-mile drive, across timeless meadows more accustomed to the clatter of hooves than internal combustion engines.

The ancient hedges, thus violated, clawed at the scarlet paint. Astonished cows lollopped to the distant ends of the fields; birds and fauna sought refuge from the cacophony of voices falsely strident in the new confidence bestowed by uniform. The foetus of an army, borne prematurely to a civilization under threat of rape by a mad Austrian ex-housepainter, had arrived in the English countryside to mature.

The buses swung left across freshly raked gravel and stopped. One behind the other they waited while the occupants peered up at the pseudo-Gothic, grey facade which had once fronted the Victorian Huxleys to what, for a priviledged few, had been a more gracious world. The bowling greens, fresh-trimmed, were vacant, but a belated tennis-foursome whom no-one had told, paused in its quadrille as the khaki invaders, like so many ants, made vague formation under the directions – not orders yet – of a highly polished officer and his underling N.C.O.s. The whole perform-

*'Huxley', John Dickinson's Sports Club turned searchlight H.Q.*

ance, product of a succession of carefree weekend camps, was amateur.

Into the uncertain hiatus there stepped a very professional figure, that of the Permanent Staff Instructor. The unit knew him well, and since the false call-up of 1938 which had preceded Chamberlain's return from Germany waving an entirely illusory piece of paper, he had been treated with a quaking sycophancy on the parade ground, but as a joke off it. He emerged now from the great porch of Huxley House as if he owned the place. Stiffly shining, for the last time in the glory of full-dress blues, he marched down the grand stone staircase; at the bottom he snapped his cane under his left arm and saluted the officer in a flurry of gravel.

Apart from a few of the older officers, batmen and technicians, who were known to have served in France, C.S.M. Taylor was the only man there with real war service. Although there had been no declaration yet, most of those who fell in under their Corporal Detachment Commanders, if not quite convinced, believed that, failing a miracle, this interruption of summer camp heralded the real thing. War was now in the air for them too, and they welcomed the emergence of authority. It afforded an illusion of refuge from something they couldn't understand.

"P'rade – P'rade Shun! As y'were!

"Para-a-de – P'rade Shun!"

All over Great Britain for the ensuing months similar preludes were being enacted, preludes to new lives for millions, death for very many thousands.

Lance Corporal John Ashley was not even sure why he was there at all.

He came to Huxley, one might say, by pure accident. A linguist of some accomplishment, after spending many years abroad with an itinerant diplomatic father and a mother of Continental education, he had worked in an office concerned with the international servicing of aircraft; but in 1938 the feeling was abroad that widespread enlistment with the Colours might convince Hitler that Britain would not lightly accept his expansionist antics. Few realised that enthusiasm was almost her only weapon. The convenient joining centre had been that provided by the Territorial Headquarters in the South London suburb where he lodged. The place had associations with his old school. There came a week when disquieting news from Europe provoked an hysterical crescendo, and John and many others like him signed up with a Searchlight Company of the Royal Engineers. The panic subsided and the "T.A." became a social club; training, a matter of attending sufficient parades to draw an annual bounty. A few were far-sighted enough to realise that an era was ending – they took the Service seriously.

When the alarm sounded anew a year later, John tried to transfer to the

**" On Active Service—Sunset to 8 o'clock."**

*A searchlight site, 1939 by the cartoonist Brian Robb.*

R.A.F., but the wheels of military bureaucracy are even more fixed in their courses than the Civil Service variety. John had, as yet, perpetrated no crime which might accelerate either his transfer or promotion by offending or impressing a superior. His request to be moved was ignored. The unit changed from peace time to full war footing while at summer camp, and here he was at Huxley, with kit bag, unauthorised suitcase, and one stripe, in charge of a Telephone Control Room which he didn't even know existed.

He'd never seen a switchboard nor operated a field telephone, and his ears were not suitable for sound locater work. The mysteries of the arc circuit in a searchlight were quite beyond him, but he wasn't unintelligent.

He was installed in the attic of Huxley House with the batmen and mess waiters. There wasn't much room, but the batmen had set up bedside tables made of orange boxes between the straw-filled palliasses. By the time John arrived there were already two pin-ups on the wall, one of Fay Wray and the other unknown, and an optimist had written "Grosvenor House" on a large card and nailed it over the door.

He dropped his kit on the only vacant palliasse, and by virtue of his one stripe, asked Jock, the C.O.'s very senior but friendly batman, if he'd mind drawing his three blankets from stores. Then he reported to Company Office.

The place was in confusion. The office staff sat at two trestle tables, a Sergeant, a Corporal and a Sapper, with the vague accoutrements of their peacetime cubbyhole in Wimbledon transplanted in disarray about them. Under one table someone was trying to get some sleep. The C.O., Major Gosport, and two other officers, all issued directions and paid much attention to a new map, marked off in sections, pinned awkwardly to a blackboard, relic of a sportsclub briefing session. The P.S.I., now rationally clad in first-war khaki service dress, but still flourishing a cane with a silver knob, confounded the bedlam by striding back and forth through everything as if he were on parade.

"Sergeant," ventured the Major, who hadn't yet fully found his military voice after years in an office, "Take Corporal Ashley down to the Control Room, would you. See if you can get wired up, Corporal. Staff Q hasn't got here yet so you'll have to do the best you can. Know anything about telephones?" And then the Major was distracted by a piercing summons from his own single outside 'phone. John Ashley's protestation of ignorance was lost in the rush of the Orderly Sergeant's boots and he was whisked away down a flight of stone steps into what had once been a section of the Huxley wine cellar, which now, in spite of the pristine billiards table which still stood in it, was about to become the nerve centre of a considerable segment of London's hastily contrived anti-aircraft defences.

"The map's over there, Corporal," said the Sergeant, vaguely waving in the general direction of a copy of the area diagram which had graced the blackboard in the Orderly Room, "and this is the concentrator." Or the Never-Never Land, reflected John, as a rush of boots magicked him away.

In the ensuing silence John wondered about his own boots. Did they make that much racket? It's true boots were important in a soldier's life, all that heel-ball and spit and polish. Still, you felt good when you were well turned out, and he chuckled to himself as he remembered his first day in uniform just a year ago; Jock had bent the peak of his cap down like a guardsman's; it made you keep your head up. He'd done just that, and walked straight into a lamppost, to the amusement of several passers-by who wouldn't have noticed him otherwise. This interlude just couldn't be really happening. Any moment now the alarm would go, he'd wake up, and have to get dressed and go to the office. But when he moved, the boots were only too real.

John examined the map, but obsessional security had removed from it anything which might relate to the overall geography of what he knew to be Hertfordshire.

He stared hard at the concentrator. Something had to be done about that. "Get wired up." the C.O. had said. The evil-looking box affair with rows of up-and-down switches seemed to stare back in the silence. John flicked them with no result.

He opened a cupboard behind the door, but shut it again quickly. It was full to bursting with what appeared to be discarded female undergarments of ample dimensions. For some ridiculous reason he felt himself blushing – he was a very innocent young man. The next cupboard exposed the scurrying retreat of a surprised rat, which seemed unwilling to go. That door hadn't been opened in years. He climbed on a chair to explore the picture rail and some high shelves, and succeeded only in obtaining the weakest of electric shocks from the last remnant of the Huxley complex of servants' bells. The wire, which crumbled in his hand, had long since borne summons to its last skivvy. It couldn't possibly animate a communications centre.

At length, John opened a window facing a railed area below what appeared to be the drive, for he could just glimpse through it the bottom of a large wheel, probably a bus. Fresh air wafted into the close cellar, and there, hanging down from nowhwere, were some cables, including one with a multiple plug. The G.P.O. at least had known what it was about. He pulled the plug into the room and then discovered a female counterpart in the back of the concentrator. The holes matched. With a muttered prayer that the whole contrivance would not blow up, he pushed the big plug home. So far, so good. He donned the headset, sat down, flicked the first switch and turned the little handle.

"Duty Officer," said a surprised voice.

"Control Room testing," said John, equally surprised, but trying to conceal it.

"Who's that speaking?" asked the Duty Officer, as if he'd been expecting a call from Julius Caesar.

"Lance Corporal Ashley, sir. I've just connected up."

"Very good work, Corporal," said the officer, for whom nothing at all had so far gone to plan. "I'll tell the C.O. He'll be pleased because we didn't expect to be connected until this evening. Keep up the good work."

John tried all the other switches, reported in turn to the C.O., the Officers' Mess, the Sergeants' Mess and the Company Office. He received surprised congratulations from all of them and each said he'd tell the others. The C.O. told him to stay where he was until he was relieved. The big box died for several hours, then occasional calls started coming through and John, after a few mistakes, which he found provoked a rather special type of entirely unjustified telephone ire, discovered how to hold and pass them on. Someone thought he was the Police Station and wanted to report a lost dog, and when he found that he couldn't say who he was without disclosing his location and breaking security regulations, he noted down the owner's name, the dog's name and details of where it might have strayed. He had connected up before any of the other Units had even started to set up their equipment. John took a cue from the rack and tried a few cannons on the billiards table. When that palled he slept on it, dead beat, in spite of the chilly slate, having of course, first removed his boots.

He was still there the following morning when someone remembered him when he wasn't on parade. He hadn't had anything to eat since midday the day before, and even telephonists must be rested. The C.O., conscience-stricken, sent him a belated breakfast from the Officers' Mess at ten o'clock. Parades can be useful.

The C.O. was very conscientious. He courted popularity, assiduously concealing his peacetime occupation as manager of a firm of manure distributors. John Ashley received his second stripe the following day. It was only later that he discovered, from one of the outlying section clerks behind the voices on his now jealously possessed new toy, the concentrator, that two stripes no longer made a Corporal. Someone, somewhere deep in the War Office, had decided that searchlights should be operated, not by Sappers, but Gunners. The 30th Battalion Royal Engineers became the 30th Regiment, Royal Artillery, with Batteries instead of Companies, with permission to continue wearing the Sappers' blancoed lanyard; and they could, on suitable occasions, still sing the Engineers' vocal souvenir of the War in South Africa, the "C.R.E."

On the whole, as a member of 290 Battery, John approved. A Bombardier sounded more impressive than a Corporal and these things matter a great deal when one is young.

It is in the nature of things that military formations, once they settle, immediately fall into routine. You can't run an Army "doing your own thing". Three days later Bombardier Ashley had a Lance Jack and a Gunner to share his labours. He had adopted an authoritarian telephone voice to snap out, in rote, the questions columned in the sundry piles of Returns which had to be completed at regular times and intervals. When he called, the telephonists on Section sat to attention with their information. That was his fond hope. The cookhouse sent down meals liberally garnished with Officers' and Sergeants' tit-bits by grace of the occupants of "Grosvenor House". Before John Ashley's newly established, comfortable world blew up in his face, most of the Unit listened one morning to the Sergeants' Mess wireless set, as Chamberlain, he of the "Umberella", made his only immortal speech. Having placed a deliberately impossible withdrawal ultimatum upon the committed Reich, he confirmed what everyone said they knew already. England was at war with Germany.

At what might just as well have been the other end of the world, some days after Lance Corporal John Ashley blossomed as an electrical genius, Janet Oldfield hurried home in the new blackout to the large flat in Chiswick where she lived with her step-parents, to pack the few belongings that an A.T.S. volunteer was permitted to take away to war. Hurrying had become relative to the new situation, well-known landmarks having disappeared. Shopfronts became darkly anonymous in the blackout. Familiar lampposts were obstacles, not beacons, and gateposts were hazards.

Janet was small and blonde, twenty, and wise to the ways of the world by courtesy of the rag trade and the Young Conservatives. In common with many of the youth of her day, she was affronted by the evil potential building up across the Channel. She was also, in an odd, self-conscious kind of way, proud to be British, and if her sentiments were slightly confused by the rantings of Sir Oswald Mosely, and the curious, introspective mutterings of the pacifists, at least she was sufficiently imbued with an instinct for adventure to do exactly as John Ashley had done. She also had signed a paper, had taken a leap out of the suburban rut and would report to Territorial Headquarters on the morrow. Like a parcel with no address she was due for onward despatch, and wondered, slightly apprehensively, whither. A number of people asked themselves the same question before the night was out.

John Ashley was on duty at his switch board. The billiard table had been stowed away. The map had been coloured by the Lance Jack, who was ambitious. There were more chairs, and two beds for off-duty personnel. A primitive rack over the switchboard now bore a row of hooks for the daily Return forms. The buzzers had been silent since nine o'clock and John was writing a letter.

Suddenly one of the outside lines vibrated into life. A rattle of female incoherence spat in John's ear.

"You anti-aircraft?"

Security was beginning to bite. You just didn't answer questions like that not even on a Service Telephone line. Careless talk cost lives, but the Cockney twang didn't smack of Hitler.

"Who are you?"

"Huxley Exchange 'ere," said the voice, realising the moment – one to be savoured – and, damn security, one to be talked about. "Look. I got a lady ringing from Cromer. Says there's an air raid comin'. What'll I do with 'er?"

"Put her on," said John. And thus, with the observers out on the coast and listening posts and searchlights peppering the land from the Eastern and Southern limits of the country to London, the first air raid warning came from a little old lady in Cromer, all the way to Huxley. She thought she heard an aeroplane.

John passed the details to the Duty Officer, dozing, fully dressed, on one of the beds. He straightened his Sam Browne and summoned the C.O. The C.O. put on the spare headset, called out the guard and stood-to all the lights. The machine gunners on site manned their first-war Lewis guns and checked the half pan of ammunition. The single rifle carried by some detachment sentries got one up the spout, and somewhere, somewhere which was a secret, a few – no-one now remembers how few, very experimental Spitfires scrambled. The Home Guard all round London manned road blocks, pick-helves at the ready. Nobody thought to order the "Take Cover" for headquarters staff.

It was over in an hour, a friendly Percival Q6 belonging to a yachting millionaire had been identified on its way to Croydon Aerodrome. In all the lines of defence not a single soul had noticed the approach of an aircraft – only an old lady, probably with memories of a previous conflict, had reported it. Britain had a great deal yet to learn.

At three a.m. the line from the guard tent at the main check point on the drive suddenly came to life.

"Guard tent 'ere. That the Bombardier?" Came a hoarse whisper. "Somethin's 'appenin'. I can 'ear somethin' movin'."

"Where's the Guard Commander?"

" 'E's asleep."

"Well, wake him up. Try and do it quietly. I'll get the Duty Officer."

The sentry had been brought up in the backstreets of Hackney. To him the countryside was a place of hidden horror and mystery, particularly after dark. He heard inexplicable stirrings. Thinking that perhaps a colleague might have overstayed his late pass, he challenged.

"Halt! who goes there?" There was no response, and the movement continued to approach, slowly, relentlessly. He couldn't bring himself to fire at it.

After ringing the Control Room the sentry had gone in to wake the Guard Commander, remembering, at the crucial moment, the only fragment of country craft he ever knew from an old film. Red Indians woke each other silently by pressing under the right ear of the sleeper. In the film it had worked, but the sentry suddenly had doubts. He wasn't an Indian. To be sure, he clapped a hand over the Guard Commander's mouth as he opened his eyes. It was a dark night and the Guard Commander slumbered deeply after a few bottles of the local Benskin's strong brew. He was a Scot. He gave vent to a banshee wail which brought the Duty Officer galloping down the drive waving a pistol.

Two shamefaced figures awaited him. A Lance-Bombardier, a Gunner – and an amiable Jersey cow which had strayed from a neighbouring field.

After what he came to regard as his first night of action John retired to his palliasse – now suspended, by virtue of Jock's carpentry, upon a contrivance knocked together out of boards and sacking – in the cossetted purlieus of "Grosvenor House". The batmen and waiters, summoned from their slumbers by the various involvements of their masters in the events of the night, were earnestly expressing their adjectival opinions, freely lubricated by an early morning ration of purloined beer.

John was a teetotaller. He slept, and while he slept and dreamed of an invasion by Jersey cows with swastikas on their rumps, a lorry from a mystical transport pool, driven by a volunteer civilian on a very high rate of pay (which was why he'd volunteered), made its way uncertainly into Hertfordshire. It travelled vaguely for an obvious reason. No-one in it knew the way. The driver had been given only a diagram of the London Underground, that and a map reference. The Sergeant Major who'd seen the vehicle off said not to worry. "Keep going north, then follow the signs. Can't miss it," but the Home Guard had taken all the signs down in case the Germans landed. Which was why the lorry came at last to Watford from Wimbledon by way of Brixton and Tower Bridge.

The A.T.S. Section Leader who sat beside the driver was tired of the uncertain odyssey of the last two hours. Even the six A.T.S. volunteers, Janet Oldfield among them, who sat on garden benches in the open back of the vehicle, were getting bored with wolf whistles and the appreciative regard of the male public. They were realising what many knew already, that uniform and inhibition seldom march together. Their khaki outfits had been tastefully, if fortuitously enhanced by the issue of stylish and rather expensive civilian tweed overcoats authorised by an enthusiastic Quartermaster who had designs on the Section Leader, and who had run out of Greatcoats, Army, A.T.S., For The Use Of. The girls had taken off their caps and looked as if they were out for the day.

The descent of the party at a Carmen's Pull-Up caused a minor sensation. There was a deal of earthy banter as the Section Leader enquired the way to Huxley. "You mean the new Top Secret place up at the Sports Club, doncher?" said a large unshaven bruiser in overalls. "Six miles up the road. That's where they 'ad the warnin' las' night. Invasion they was expectin'. That's wot it were. Wasn't you sayin', Joe, as that's where they shot them cows? Only they don't say nothin' about it, see. Young Milly, you know, Syd's daughter, told me. She works the telephones. If 'tweren't fer 'er no-one'd know wot goes on!"

John Ashley came down shortly after midday to take over the afternoon shift. He'd written up a projected diary for the coming week based on the duty roster. There were places he wished to visit locally, things to do, but Army rosters tend to be subject to contingency situations, as John discovered when he came into the Control Room.

Jock was putting the final surprisingly effeminate touch to the flowers in a vase which stood on top of the concentrator. The chairs had been moved from their accustomed geometric situation and the beds were upended against the wall. The C.O., in immaculate riding breeches and spurred boots, stood, legs apart, with a pint tankard in his hand, talking to an A.T.S. Three-Striper. Another pint tankard stood before the switch-board, and a small blonde figure sat in his chair, wearing his headset.

"Ah, Bombardier," said the Major, in what John came to know as his bluffest, sell-you-a-ton-of-manure voice. "Meet our new office staff. This is Section Leader Bray, and that's Volunteer Oldfield. I want you to teach our new intake how to use the concentrator."

"The Bombardier," he added, in parenthesis to the Section Leader, "is an expert on these things. He had us connected up when we arrived here nearly six hours before anyone else had started. Gerald, the Brigadier – he's my assistant in Civvy Street, you know – was very pleased. Shall we go and finish our tour, Section Leader? – or shall I call you Daphne? We'll leave Janet to the Bombardier."

Suddenly John was left alone in a rocking world. Jock had departed with a promise to send down tea and biscuits of all things in half-an-hour. That was the first of many contrived visits to the Control Room that afternoon. Everyone wanted to see the new operator, and by the end of the day the concensus of opinion pronounced Janet "a smasher".

When it came to the crunch, John realised there wasn't much you could say about Army telephonic communication. The Returns were all labelled, with times and destinations. He'd written down the standard A – Apple, B – Brother, C – Charlie alphabet as he remembered it from his aviation days. As for the operation of the switchboard, that too was obvious. Janet was already deeply involved in a conversation with someone on a section line to whom a female voice was providing welcome relief from the day-to-day monotony of life in a field with nothing but a detachment and a fully equipped searchlight, and she held one conversation, connected two other calls meanwhile and made enquiry for the Orderly Room about a train time from Huxley without a break.

John tried to assert his authority.

"It's not usual," he said, "to drink beer in the Control Room."

Janet looked at him with grey eyes. Experienced Young Conservatives, even hardened gown salesmen, had wilted under that glance. "Well, I didn't fetch it down myself, you know. Major Gosport had it brought. Want some?"

The voice matched the eyes. "Er . . . I don't drink, I'm afraid."

John Ashley's professed standards suffered severe erosion before the day was out; he drank half the beer, and when Janet was relieved by the Lance Bombardier, who arrived hopefully half-an-hour early for his shift at 5.30, he marched arrogantly, feeling seven feet tall, with her through an envious camp, and all the two miles into Huxley Village. The austerity supper at the Green Tiles Cafe might have been a banquet. John slipped further still at "The Bell", where, later, the competition for Janet's favours was intense. John had several drinks, decided he approved of the effect and boldly proposed, since the moon was high, a walk back through the fields instead of along the road. They lingered behind the ancient churchyard where an archiac yew had provided shelter for lovers for nearly a thousand years. Not everyone cursed the maniac over the water in Europe, not all the time.

The romance blossomed and the big, temporary wartime settlement, the camp, accepted it, each adopting it as something personal, something to provide relief from invasion scares, from bombing and death, from madness. It was even reported upon in letters home.

*Auxiliary Territorial Service Volunteers, 1940. 'Janet' seated centre.*

It was Jock who cast the first shadow upon the Control Room idyll. He was too good a batman to make free of the gossip he overheard in the Officers' quarters. He liked his job, and was past active service. Most of his friends knew that he was considerably older than his record showed. So he did his job well, made himself as nearly indispensable as he could, and kept his mouth shut.

But he liked young John. John did no-one any harm. He was generous and carried his junior rank like a gentleman. He didn't throw his weight about like so many of the little dictators cast up by the country's sudden militarisation.

"Ye're in tr-rouble with the Major, John," he announced quietly one night as the Bombardier returned to his billet a few, very few minutes before the expiration of his pass. "He says, of all the daft things, that ye shouldn' be going wi' a Pr-rivate when ye've tew str-ripes yersel. He's right o'coorse aboot the discipline, but ah'd a thocht he had better-r things tae wor-ry aboot. Anywa' he's sendin' ye awa' an' givin' ye a detachment. 'Haltsford, he said. 'Tisna' far. Ye'll have tae get a bicycle, lad!"

When the posting appeared two days later in Battery Orders, the new situation was accepted philosophically by both John and Janet. There was a war on. The time for philandering was over, for the present at least.

When John moved to Haltsford, they announced their engagement. "If they want to make stupid regulations", remarked John, "we'll see what they do about that." Before he left, John, whose wages were being made up by the Aviation firm which employed him in peace-time, bought a case of beer to be shared among his friends in "Grosvenor House".

Haltsford proved to be a Section Headquarters site at which one of Britain's war-winning secrets was undergoing tests. A.R.C., John learned, faced with a daunting straggle of green painted, curiously animated and well-oiled machinery, stood for Automatic Remote Control.

A tiny, primitive radar screen, one of the first of millions of later-developed models which now direct almost all forms of remote transport, was at the heart of the contrivance. To it three huge coordinated listening trumpets indicated the course of any adjacent flying target. Instead of lying, in the traditional position, spreadeagled in a device like a tropical armchair with leg extensions and confusing stethoscope plugs like an eccentric G.P., John, as Detachment Commander, now sat high on a contraption which he described as straight out of Well's "War of the Worlds".

As the cumbersome sound locator moved, the linked mechanism of the searchlight, some fifty yards away, beyond the "Dig for Victory" vegetable patch, already several times flooded and very trampled, proceeded in

*'John Ashley' outside the O.P. in rural Hertfordshire.*

tandem. No-one had yet thought to link the anti-aircraft guns directly to the locator, thus eliminating the light altogether. The equipment was effective – in pinpointing more homecoming aircraft than raiding Germans. Returning airmen, once they passed the coast, regarded themselves as home and dry, and not knowing how trigger happy one becomes after several month's isolation in a field, often forgot to fire their Verey recognition signals.

The searchlight had a deep trench which flooded at the lightest shower round it, another inspiration of a first war strategist in case the Germans landed. On his first night of action, John's command to "Take Post" emerged as a hoarse bellow into a high wind, surprising both himself and the sentry who unexpectedly picked it up on the radar screen. There followed a near-tragedy, as the Lance-Bombardier charged with pulling the switch on the light to engage the carbons, entangled in tin hat-strap and gas mask, took a dive into three feet of muddy water which certainly hadn't been there during his last inspection.

If the Boches had arrived, the effectiveness of one rifle, five rounds of ammunition and the ten pickhelves which constituted Section armament would in any case have been doubtful.

There was of course, the Lewis-gun, mounted in solitary splendour in a circle of sand-bags. It had half a pan of ammunition, and everyone had learned, in theory at least, on Summer evenings, how to dissect it to its tiniest elements, and put them back together, in the dark, in three minutes flat.

The Lewis-gun was another 1918 relic, and it doubled as the secret weapon of a flying column in case the Section were called to the assistance of the Local Defence Volunteers. Then it was mounted on the roof of a most decrepit local taxi, the better vehicles having already been taken by other services.

The whole detachment was turned out, in its "Flying" capacity, to harass the enemy when a local firework factory sent up an experimental rocket which released a shower of tiny parachutes. They looked big through binoculars and the Observer who spotted them was short-sighted in any case.

And so a prim and rather callow youth became a man in a matter of weeks, living basically with a detachment of men from all walks of life, men who, but for the war, would never have crossed his path.

There was a little Welshman of violent disposition who hated everything. The Bombardier had to entice him down, in the early light of a freezing dawn, from the roof of his Section Hut, whither he had climbed, after a night of false air-raid alarms, threatening to kill himself, and any who climbed near, with a Norwegian sheath-knife. There was a dark-eyed gipsy who had never before settled in one place for more than a few weeks. His knowledge of field craft and wild life often helped to eke out meagre rations. There was a local postman who courted – and married Gertie, a maid at Haltsford House. A bank clerk who had been a black-shirt under Mosley, but whose mother had relatives in the Government, was the subject of obscure investigation. There was a transport contractor and an editor.

They all lived at Haltsford, which became known as "Little Venice". Their destinies, for a whole year, merged in a muddy field. Theirs was one of the probing lights which pin-pointed the raiders on the night London burned, and Cockney morale, against all reason, surged into a perverse resolve to conquer, whatever the odds. They suffered only one casualty throughout the blitz. A visiting officer, seeking to catch the sentry unawares, crept along a ditch, and was smartly laid out with a pickhelve as he approached the gate. The chin-strap of his tin hat nearly broke his neck!

In the muddiest corner of the field stood a bell tent, another World War I relic. This was the Section Observation Post, the "O.P.", which had to be manned during the hours of darkness. In it stood a folding chair and a trestle table with an extension telephone, a clip-board and a hurricane lamp upon it. In Winter a smoky Valor paraffin stove with an inadequate ration of fuel reinforced the inventory, and on it John Ashley, who, in spite of his stripes, insisted on doing his shift, discovered how to fry an egg.

On one of the coldest nights he was fortifying himself against the elements with a snack and was about to break his egg – from Hartsford Farm, for rationing was strict in the civilian world – into the frying pan, when the telephone buzzed. Field telephones didn't jangle. They merely insinuated themselves. John was practically smothered in every warm garment he owned, and encumbered by a new pair of mittens and a balaclava helmet knitted by Janet, he moved awkwardly. Catching the handle of the pan as he reached for the telephone he dropped his egg directly onto the top of the Valor.

There, as John dealt with an enquiry about rations, it sizzled weakly for an instant before slithering slowly through the circle of holes down upon the burning wick.

There immediately issued forth a cloud of evil-smelling smoke and John had to spend the rest of the night cleaning up. Only towards dawn did he finish writing his nightly effusion to Janet. They wrote each other long letters, even though John usually contrived to be on hand whenever returns were passed, whenever, that is, he knew that Janet was to be on duty at H.Q.

The egg in the stove produced a sequel. The following day there was a thaw. Normal smells were obscured by a lingering aroma of incinerated egg and paraffin. And in the next field, beyond the hedge by the O.P., was a rotting haystack, forgotten in the exigencies of war. The thaw confounded an already confused aromatic night.

That very morning Major Gosport had circulated a warning on Gas. The first World War kept poking meddling fingers into the Second. There were several gasses, it seemed, but the only one John remembered was phosgene, and that smelled of "rotting hay". Having endured agonies of indecision in the O.P., John finally summoned up his courage at 9.55, just before Janet went off duty, and issued the only Gas Alert of World War II.

Everyone smiled. Love had odd symptoms, and the Major's conspiracy to prevent improper mingling between the ranks was seen to have failed miserably.

There came Dunkirk, a huge defeat celebrated with Anglo-Saxon perversity as glorious victory because the underdog got away to fight again. Then rumour, many-handed, of thwarted invasion, tales of scorched cadavers seen, always from a distance, because the guards prevented you from going close, bobbing in the waves off Margate, or Southend or the Isle of Wight.

John's bed at Huxley was taken over by a new batman, another Welsh conscript, who looked after two very new and young lieutenants. Conscripted armies cast their nets broadly, bringing in quantity rather than quality. In the peacetime Territorials each unit tended to be drawn from a fairly level social stratum. Business groups, school years, sports clubs, they joined up together, anticipating a short, sharp conflict and a quick release back into the civilian pool. Few foresaw the vague and distant paths many of them would be forced to tread. Even now, after only a few months of progressive mobilisation, the initial friendly structure was being penetrated by intakes from elsewhere. Little bands of Welsh miners found themselves among bank clerks. Gipsies appeared among civil servants and salesmen. Commercial artists discussed social affairs with dustmen.

Taffy Jones knew himself by none of the acceptable army classifications. The recruiting officer, another misfit, had put him at the bottom of a list for the Pioneer Corps, but when the new intake came to depart the lorry wasn't big enough. Taffy was left over and sent to Huxley.

Obviously he had never been a batman. He was too young to have had any experience in that direction. He spent a lot of time scrounging both material and advice from Jock and the others, and batmen are notoriously jealous, both of their secrets and their possessions. Fortunately, Taffy's new masters, never having had a personal servant before, were neither observant nor demanding, so Taffy lasted several weeks before achieving the pinnacle of his army career. He eventually became Headquarters Latrine Orderly, in which capacity he alternated with a disreputable and obstinate Peer of the Realm who refused, under any circumstances to wear socks, thus putting paid to any chance of military advancement, otherwise, who knows, he might have become a General. The C.S.M. enjoyed announcing, after saluting smartly the Duty Officer on visiting rounds, that all the sanitation complaints would be referred forthwith to Sir Owen.

Meanwhile Taffy was not happy. He tried drinking in the village, even offering to chip in with an occasional round, but he found both the natives and the khaki immigrants obsessed with an almost blinkered sense of occupational possession. They weren't going to accept willingly any intrusion into the social "perks" they had already achieved, and which many locals were begining to regret.

Taffy was invariably left isolated at one end of the bar. Patrolling Military Police tended to stop him and criticise his turnout. When he attempted conversation with a local farmer, he found that Swansea and Huxley might just as well have been Timbuctoo and Toronto.

So he tried a new road to relaxation. Instead of joining the evening exodus, now reinforced by several privately owned vehicles, down the Drive to Huxley Village, Taffy prospected the back of Huxley House. From what had once been the servants' wing, a path led to a stile and a pathway across a paddock. Here Taffy found himself on top of a hill with a vast green panorama spreading ahead. He had never seen a prospect so bereft of slag-heaps. Another rise with another large building on top of it beckoned. Taffy decided to investigate.

The square pile he looked at, Raymead, had been there since before Queen Anne, as had the well-beaten track which connected it with the old Huxley, and now led to its successor. It stood in open wheat and barley fields, with large paddocks where the family hunters had passed a very pleasant existence. The present family, the Fosters, like the Wilkinsons, had made a fortune out of paper. They didn't ride hard, but they liked their horses.

The horses had been boxed off to Cornwall. The younger Fosters had joined up. The over-young and the elderly, excepting for one superannuated survival of the Boer War who insisted upon moving to London to join the Auxiliary Fire Service, followed the horses. When Taffy first came to Raymead, old James Massey was away for an evening's cinema relaxation, so he had the place to himself.

James Massey, home from the sea, had at first enjoyed his temporary caretaking duties. His own savings, and the money inherited from his brother, Adam, were safely invested. He travelled, played golf, joined a few clubs, and only very occasionally remembered the squalid little cottage in Streatham. Seldom, when all the Fosters were away from Raymead together, and that wasn't often while the children were growing up, was he obliged to remain for long at Huxley.

But the War had brought change. James's older contemporaries had died. Then his house in Hampstead received a direct hit. He took all his surviving belongings, including many things bequeathed by Adam, out of the Army and Navy Depositary and moved permanently down to Raymead, where he took up residence in a flat in the west wing. He was able to tell his envious club-mates that he had a little place on the Hertfordshire Downs.

At seventy-five he was still very active, thinking of getting married again to a Vicar's widow who lived in the village.

All that was beyond the ken of Taffy. First of all he sauntered casually. The windows of the house, from a distance, looked redly blind to the setting sun. There was no obvious sign of occupation, but Taffy still took care over an operation which, to him, was apparently routine. To anyone who might have been watching, he looked as if he were passing Raymead by, a soldier out for an evening stroll.

As it grew darker he turned back upon the place from behind, moving now silently and with extreme caution. No-one saw him shin smartly over the old red brick wall into the courtyard, nor heard him slip like a shadow across it.

People who live in the country trust their neighbours. The first window Taffy tried opened to his touch. He didn't have to use his blackout torch or any of the compact set of tools in his pocket. In the gloaming he dropped quietly into a great scullery, even his booted feet making little sound upon the old, worn pantiles. Raymead had never been burgled before, and Taffy, who may have had the qualities attributed to him in an old nursery rhyme, was also a tactician. He knew that he was in no situation to dispose of great quantities of loot. He didn't know the fences hereabouts anyway. If he helped himself carefully to things that were not obvious, at the same time remaining in legitimate employment at Huxley, he could do very well for himself.

He looked about, using now the torch, from which he had removed the rubber shield with the slit decreed by blackout regulations. He entered a long dim corridor and came into a large square room where the beam picked up cabinets of porcelain figures, but he recognised from the careful arrangement of everything that they were regularly washed and tended. He did consider taking two pieces from right at the back of one cabinet, but decided against them. There was a goldmine here. As long as he remained at Huxley he could come back again and again. He would play a waiting game. He decided to leave the main building for another visit.

In the kitchen he came upon the kind of cache he was really seeking, in the room off the one where he had made his first entry. He found there a place, which, from its condition, was obviously not regularly cleaned or scrubbed. Right at the back of the bottom cupboard of a great Welsh dresser he discovered a heap of copper utensils. They had been stowed away when there was no-one any longer to labour with lemon and salt to keep them clean. On the front of the deep shelf, blacker than the nesting saucepans, stood a tea-pot, milk jug and sugar basin, and Taffy's acquaintance with the nefarious market in "bent" silver, had taught him that such things are seldom made of copper. He knew of plate, of course, but that tends to look heavy, and even the criminal mind can recognise elegance. Smiling broadly to himself in the dark as he picked up his trophies, he blew dust over the patches left by the three pieces, and casually departed for his new home, quietly shutting the window behind him.

He tried to clean the silver tea set with some Brasso he found with the button-stick, polishes and Blanco by Jock's bed when he got back. By that time he had identified a hall-mark. Jock caught him at it and was furious, but Taffy, in his way, was diplomat as well as strategist. He let the storm die down. Then he told a touching tale of seeing the pieces in a junk shop, of remembering the talk he'd heard of Janet and John's budding romance.

"Look you, for three poun', man. It'd make a fine wedding present, don' you think?"

Jock stopped short in full verbal flight. Taffy was right. Three Pounds. There were twelve of them in "Grosvenor Hoouse." That made five bob each.

John and Janet remained undeterred by Major Gosport's attempt to enforce his interpretation of King's Regulations in the matter of mixing among the ranks. With two hired bicycles of ancient vintage, on their rare coinciding leave periods, they covered the neighbouring countryside with astonishing diligence. They rented a room in the village from a sympathetic school-master's wife, and for nearly a year, while the hounds of war bared their teeth and snarled across Europe, they existed in a world of their own.

Such an idyll had to end, of course. Major Gosport returned one day from an HQ briefing bristling with importance. From then onwards there appeared a new purpose in the Unit's activities. Little was said, but by dint of hint and rumour the secrets of the Orderly Room filtered through

Sections and Detachment Commanders to the ranks. The 30th Searchlights were for Overseas.

Janet, at her privileged post in the Control Room, heard the news early. With a moistness of eye and a fortitude of which only a short year ago she knew she would have been incapable she kept her secret for two whole days, but when John met her in the village on a cold Friday evening, she sobbed bitterly.

"You might never come back, John. This could go on for years."

John, himself bursting with news of a prospective promotion, was deflated. "I'll come back if it lasts ten years, Jan." He paused. "When's your birthday?"

"Two weeks, and I'll be twenty-one."

"Right, and you say that we move at the end of the month? Then there'll be embarkation leave and maybe a few other delays. Tell you what, let's get married."

In spite of Janet's token protest, a few days later, two perfectly casual villagers were stopped in the street by a starry-eyed couple in khaki. In spite of an air-raid warning they agreed to go to the Registrar's Office to witness a marriage contract. The Registrar thought of taking cover, but something about the young couple, the look in Janet's eyes perhaps, caused him to ignore the ominous thrumming overhead.

The silver tea set was the best present they received, for there was little time to notify relatives. Even the C.O., after a deal of pompous ranting in the Mess about the unsuitability of war-time weddings, wished them well.

In a month, the unit moved to Fleetwood, marched down the main street, and was billetted in twos, house by house, upon the friendly Lancastrians. Janet spent her honeymoon there.

When John finally sailed for the Middle East, Janet returned to the concentrator with a new Unit. She put the tea set, for safe keeping, in the bottom of the chest of drawers in her bedroom at her step-parent's flat. Her bedroom was on the corner of the building, the corner which received a direct hit on one of the worst nights of the London blitz.

She had other things on her mind. Sergeant John Ashley had been wounded at Mersah Matruh and she hadn't heard from him for weeks.

# Totter's Teapot

On wet, cold days, when even Nellie got frost on her whiskers, Bert wished he wasn't a totter. On fine days, when the sun shone and everyone was in good humour it was different, then he wouldn't be doing anything else. Criss cross, up and down the blocks, just an occasional clang on the bell or a half-hearted "Rag-a-bone". There was usually at least one door open on each street. Bert knew the district like the back of his hand, more about the inhabitants too than most of them realised. You learned a lot from people's junk.

You never knew quite what was coming. A bundle of rags here, old books there, a gas stove, bits of carpet. A few new pence, which he still translated into bobs and tosheroons, paid for a cart load and then you spent the rest of the day sorting. Often he didn't have to pay at all.

The little back yard in Battersea would disappear soon. It lay at the back of Victoria Walk, a row of small houses surviving the nineteenth century between two L.C.C. tower blocks. Many of their inhabitants had been named Smith or Penfold. Gipsy names, those, Pikies who had left the road and settled. Only two of the row of stables beyond the yard remained. The rest had been absorbed by a shopping centre and the manager of the supermarket there took exception to Bert's junk piles.

He was looking over the fence today when Bert led the horse and cart to the back gate. Bert doffed his old cap. " 'Afternoon, Mr Smithers," he said. It paid to keep in with the neighbours.

Mr Smithers sniffed. Bert, poker-faced and muttering under his breath, thumped Nellie's chest with one hand while appearing to stroke her nose with the other. Horse and cart smartly retreated two feet. Several yards of rusty guttering waved in Mr Smither's face and he retired with a "tut" and a despairing glance at the heavens. "Toffee nosed bastard," said Bert, and set about unloading.

The rags, wool on one side, cotton on the other, went into the lean-to to be kept dry. The iron was stacked. It didn't fetch much. The lead

*Criss, cross, up and down the blocks*

was different. You got money for that and bronze. The rest had to be considered.

Totters, like the best antique dealers in Bond Street, have channels. Between that gamut of cart to ultimate customer lies the success measure of dealers of any kind. There is a trade hierarchy, and most men and women who are not purely amateur dabblers operating only upon lucky hunches, know their own price stratum. All try not to drop and make a loss, but the lowest are not inhibited from trying to aim as high as possible.

Chairs, or bookshelves, or small tables, even old gramophones that you once broke up, were worth money now, and you had to try for the best price. It was always possible to come down, but you couldn't go up.

A good day was Friday, when you loaded the cart with particular care and headed for Bermondsey. The casual disorder of Nellie's burden was artfully contrived. You had to make it look as if you were loaded with fresh purchases even when some of the stuff had been around for years. If you had only one end of a brass bed you arranged it up front and casually left one half of an iron one showing. A Persian carpet with a hole in it had to be cunningly revealed with only a corner hanging down. The odd jerry was a good draw. It somehow showed that you'd cleared a house right down to the basics.

If the load was right you seldom reached the market, except with an empty cart for a cup of tea. Americans, who thought they were outsmarting their English colleagues, were suckers for a well-displayed load.

As you dallied in the approaches, a Transatlantic assault would take different forms. Nellie might receive a tentative pat, and she'd stop and sigh windily. "How much the platter?" or the chamber-pot, or the carpet.

Getting down had to be a laborious affair and before attending to the customer you made a show of inspecting one of Nellie's shoes; it all helped the image. In Milwaukee, over the cocktails, "where did you find that be-autiful lamp, Elmer?"

"Oh, the Dresden vayse? We bought that one in Bermondsee in London, England. There was this old man who was so worried about his horse." It sounded classy, as if you'd bought a gold bracelet in Monte Carlo. Trouble was, most Yanks came over now on the never-never. The tourists hadn't much money and even the dealers rarely carried cash. They either offered cheques or wanted a shipper to pay on collection.

If Friday was unsuccessful you could try Portobello on Saturday, and there were always the streets where the dealers congregated – Church Street, Kings Road, Westbourne Grove. Go down any of those with the cart and the odds were on someone stopping you – not, of course, near their own shops; they didn't like to be seen buying off a cart – and asking, "how much?" You opened your mouth. You started anywhere, as the mood took you. Then they made an offer, usually half what they were prepared to pay. They knew you hadn't paid a lot, and all that mattered to you was making a living.

A few things were different – very few, these days – because the telly, particularly that idiot man with the bird in a cage, had wised all the mugs and even the kids were on to the racket. Anything old was worth money, that's what people thought now, so you didn't get much that was special. The odd bit of china still turned up, Crown Derby sometimes. The Pikies and fairground people liked that, but even they were changing. Time was when they carried a bag of sovereigns. He hadn't seen a tasty piece of Dresden in years.

Silver? Bert had almost forgotten what that looked like . . . looked like. Bert was getting on. He wasn't as mentally agile as he had been. His mind had stuck in a groove like an old gramophone record.

He was squatting on a cut-down tea chest – you couldn't even get those now, tea came in plastic bags. Before him on the ground was the cardboard wine carton in which he currently kept the odd plate his meagre buying kitty produced. There was the tantalus without bottles, the partial cruet which looked alright against the wall, the old knives and forks no-one wanted, a spoon warmer shaped like a shell in soft metal, a bundle of knife rests and a bent teapot. The teapot had produced the mental block.

Nellie stamped. Bert went and slipped on her nosebag. The old mare eyed him reproachfully; there was better feed in the stable, but she knew her master. Bert had something on his mind, she'd make do with oats for the moment.

Bert returned to the teapot. It was very dented. He tentatively put a horny, cracked finger inside and tried to press it back into shape. He rubbed it on his sleeve. Then he found what he thought was a silver mark, a lion first, then a king's head. Here was matter for deep reflection.

Presently he rose and unharnessed Nellie. He gave her a quick rub down, led her into the stable and checked her feed. He called next door and told his neighbour, a retired gardener, that he might be away till tomorrow. He gave him the key to the padlock on the stable.

Since the bathroom was occupied by a large three piece suite, Bert washed and shaved with his old cutthroat over the kitchen sink. He polished his army boots and changed his suit. Then, carefully selecting a few pound notes from the cash box under the loose floor boards in the bedroom, he put them in his pocket and sallied forth, a new man behind the gold Albert on his waistcoat, to the bus stop. The teapot was in a plastic carrier.

Bert was off to see a friend, a porter in a saleroom in Kent. He didn't like London salerooms. They looked down their noses at you, particularly those hoity-toity young women.

* * *

The saleroom was established in what had once been the village hall. It had almost lost its identity now, urban development having shifted focus from the green with the church on one side, and the group of cottages on the other, to the site of the old Hall which had been demolished in the thirties.

Only a smother of red brick and Clayburne Avenue now marked the old estate. "Tasteful" Elizabethan beams and ultra-modern glass fronts and porches jostled each other. The ancient "Coach and Horses" with its sixteenth century tradition of hospitality accepted with uncomfortable grace a chain-brewer's facelift and a discotheque next door. A typical village rape in the name of progress.

Relics of earlier years still filtered with surprising frequency into the old village hall. The sales in Paxham were well publicised, a fact not entirely without notice among those who studied the antique market. There are items in the art repertoire of questionable provenance; some which for one reason or another are best not exposed immediately to the harsh light of the West End. The Duccio painting which the London experts refused to recognise for reasons of internal rivalry was sold to a European in Paxham

Auction Room for a great deal of money. International controversy is healthy for the Art Trade.

The resulting publicity had brought a flood of attractive property from well beyond the Kentish border. Recently a set of chairs had achieved mention in the national press, so buyers were likely to appear from far and wide. They found a great deal of junk, of course, but there were often good things too. Sometimes they made high prices, but occasionally the odd bargain slipped through, particularly among the items beyond Charlie's ken.

Charlie was head porter, had been for twenty years. Before that, for twenty more, after his family had moved to the country from Battersea's Victoria Walk, he had worked in various rising capacities for the firm of Gribble, Funnel and Duck, Estate Agents, Auctioneers and Valuers. The firm's offices flanked the village hall on one side, while the cottage, occupied by Charlie, provided symmetry on the other.

Of the original triumvirate of Gribble, Funnel and Duck, only a shadow remained, a Gribble grandson. He had once been scornfully dismissed, during a saleroom altercation, as a mere duckling, but real Funnels and Ducks there were now none. Horace Gribble was fond of telling anyone who would listen, of his family's illustrious auction history, conveniently ignoring what even elderly Paxhamites had almost forgotten, his upbringing as a cattle auctioneer, a real "barker". He told anyone interested, that the Emperor Caligula (he was Roman, of course) wielded the first ivory hammer. He was bent on social advancement of the wrong kind, went to the noisiest clubs, and at forty was settled into a groove of suburban complacency. He left his younger partners to handle the lucrative monotony of property dealing in a growth area. Charlie more or less ran the saleroom, prepared the catalogue with a facility born of long practice, and provided Horace with a monthly opportunity to appear in glory on the rostrum.

The last Friday sale, a successful one for Charlie since he had pocketed quite a handsome sum in commission tips, was four days gone. The hall was almost empty, only a couple of lots, two monumental wardrobes, remaining unsold, and the rest, small pieces only, neatly packed in boxes for collection by various shippers. New goods would not be arriving in quantity for at least a week. Charlie had spent the morning in his garden, waging war on the earwigs among the dahlias. His garden was a picture.

The single decker bus that crossed Paxham Green hourly did not often stop at the request sign by St Peter's Church. A stop usually meant the arrival of an American brass rubber after Sir Vincent Clayburne in the church, in which case they still had quite a walk to the Vicarage, or that the

Vicar's wife was back from shopping in the nearby Town. On view and sale days the service was reinforced. Today the bus pulled up, and those who observed such things, like Mrs Perkins at the newsagents, wondered. She was interested to see a grey-haired, blue-suited figure, dismount somewhat stiffly and stride across the grass toward the hall. Charlie, about to go inside, looked casually towards the unexpected visitor and paused. He took off his glasses, wiped them and looked again. It couldn't be.

Old men are not given to overt emotion, but mature roots grow deep. Long forgotten common adventures in the streets of Battersea more than half a century ago rendered the two old friends almost speechless.

"Charlie!"

"Bert!"

"Come on in! It's been a long time, Bert. Lookin' well. 'Ave you retired yet, or are you still . . . mm . . . dealing?"

"Still the 'orse an' cart, Charlie. Too late ter change now. They'll be pullin' the 'ouse dahn soon an' the Cahncil's wantin' ter put us in flats. Won't be room for no 'orse then, but she's gettin' on a bit anyway. Eighteen Nellie is nah. Shan't get annuver."

Charlie produced a bottle of beer. "Want some bread 'n' cheese?" The frosted old heads shed years as they talked.

"Remember the landmine on the corner, Charlie, the day you come 'ome on leave when the aucshun was shut in the war? Was finking abaht that when they pulled the last of the sheds dahn at the end of the street. Old Joe, 'im wot 'ad the reserved occupashun wiv the undertakers an' didn' join up. They fahnd 'is bowler 'at on that roof. All they ever did find!"

"An' remember Sam?"

"Which one? The chippy, or the one with the goldfish?"

"Nah, not them. Sam wot went inside for forg'ry, signin' cheques after 'e'd learned from puttin' Queen 'Lizabeth's monica on old papers. 'E carved a knife 'andle into a coach in clink an' sold it ter Queen Mary when 'e come aht. Wot wus 'is name? Ramage, that wus it. Pitcher of 'im there wus, in the Daily Mirror, showin' 'im wiv the old Queen in Portabella. She didn' know 'e'd jus' come art o' chokey!" The ensuing silence, as they remembered, did not last long.

"Life's changed, Bert."

"Suppose the building's gone where the sweet shop was, where we used to spend the farthings. Big Vantas thing on the counter for cream soda – that was a ha'penny. Stank of aniseed an' liquorice. Remember? Jam jars 'n' bottles in the back yard. Over the fence 'n' help yourself, sell 'em back to the old lady at the front 'n' spend the money in the shop. Had a bob or two, she did. Know what? When you think about it I reckon she knew what we was up to."

"Democracy, true democracy, that's wot it was, Charlie. Life 'as changed, that's fer sure. Can't do a 'and's turn nah wivart the bloomin' Cahncil or someone from the ruddy Welfare stickin' their noses in. 'Ad a young woman the uvver day said I oughter be in a 'ome. Smithers, 'im at the supermarket says the yard ain't sanit'ry. Las' week there was a young feller wantin' VAT records. VAT, I ask yer – an me a penshener wiv a bus pass. The old days was best, Charlie."

Into the hour that followed there passed a panorama of near-forgotten characters and places. The pawn shop on the corner, where the toffs from across the river came with their "tom-foolery" so as not to be recognised, the school marms and coppers, the tramps and traders, even the horses, dogs and women, Saturday night bioscopes for a penny, the thrills of the market, the scenario of long-gone Cockney-land paraded, garnished by memory, sweetened by man's facility to recall only the happy times.

The light was already failing when Bert remembered why he had come.

"I got a bit wot I think's good, Charlie," he said, picking up his plastic bag. "It's a bit bent. I don' want ter flog it fer nothin'. How would it go under the 'ammer?"

Charlie said, "I don't want no bent gear."

Bert laughed. "Not that kind o' bent, Charlie. Wouldn' do nuffink like that to an ol' friend. No, it's a bit bashed, that's all. Would it sell like that?"

Charlie surveyed the battered wreck. "It's silver alright, and it's only dented. Don't think there're any holes." He picked it up, lifted the lid and peered inside. No light showed. "It's a Bateman pot too – Hester. If we can get it back into shape perhaps we can get quite a good price. Want me to play?"

"Wotcher mean, play?"

"There's something I've wanted to do for years, Bert. I read once that the Japanese have a way of getting dents out of metal pots with rice. They seal it up inside with water and the swelling rice pushes out the dents. A damp cargo of rice'll burst the sides of a ship. That's a round pot. Should push it into shape."

"Cor!" said Bert. He was apprehensive. He didn't want his pot ruined, but the preliminaries looked harmless enough. Charlie put a piece of tin over the grill at the bottom of the spout, filled the pot with rice and added water. Then the two friends set about tying down the lid, no easy matter. The thing finished up as an untidy parcel, and just to make sure, they wrapped it all up in a blanket and left it at the end of the garden with a large stone from the rockery solidly on top. "Better not leave it in the sitting room 'case it explodes," explained Charlie with a tentative air which added nothing to Bert's peace of mind.

But the trick worked. The following morning Bert could hardly believe his eyes. Abroad early, the two friends removed the stone and eagerly opened the parcel. As the lid was untied it popped open with a hiss and the swollen rice spilled out, but the pot was unharmed, the dents had all disappeared. It was round and symmetrical as on the day when it left the Bateman workshop in 1784. Then it was just a matter of plate powder and elbow grease.

At last the pristine teapot stood on the table among the beer bottles, elegant and mellow, the bright-cut setting off the practical eighteenth century design. Bert was inclined to take it back home, he didn't want to be parted from it.

"You say that pot was made by a woman, Charlie? All that time ago? Not wot you'd understand from the 'istory books, is it, women makin' things. Wonder wot she was like?"

"Dunno," said Charlie. "There's not much about her in the books I've looked at. Some say she was just like a book-keeper, looking after the accounts and counting the shekels. There's lots about those old times'd make interesting reading if anyone could find out, but don't worry about it, Bert. It's a good teapot that, by any reckoning, an' the date mark's clear enough – 1784 I make it."

"How much'll it bring, Charlie?"

"Depends on who comes down, Bert. It's unusual to see a Bateman pot quite that shape and you might not ever find the matching jug and bowl. But it should make at least two hundred if we catalogue it right and the boys don't get at it with their Ring; but I'll be there to bid up, so don't worry. It should make a very good price with a bit of luck."

"You say two 'undred. Yer do mean two 'undred quid?"

Bert went home to Nellie without the teapot. He pondered, in the bus, about what he would do with the proceeds. A holiday? He didn't think so. There were a few hundred quid already under the floor boards. Buy a car? He'd have to learn to drive. He dozed off without reaching a decision.

A fortnight later, Charlie was busy. The saleroom was full again. One of the old local houses had disgorged its contents following the death of the owner. A warehouse lot of frustrated export furniture for Australia which had been in store for several years, had come down from the Midlands, and several good items, like Bert's teapot, had arrived from different sources to provide interest. It should be a good sale. Charlie completed the catalogue notes and retired to his garden with a sigh of satisfaction.

The following morning Horace Gribble sat in his office looking sourly at

*An early 20th century song-sheet.*

*Gribble, Funnel & Duck? Actually Reeves of Croydon.*

the incoming mail tray. He didn't like it. The day before he had visited a public relations firm in London and there he had seen an office which made his own operations centre appear paltry. The latest in Italian furniture, exotic plants, slick modern paintings and smart receptionists. The fact that his own furnishings were good, largely the product of Gribble, Funnel and Duck's activities down the years, the partners' desk from the Hall, the chairs from the old vicarage, the ornaments commemorating the progressive dismemberment of a gracious way of living, did nothing to sweeten his mood.

He rang for his secretary, and the elderly Mrs Belman, who had worked for his father, entered with homely efficiency and sat with pencil poised. Horace commenced dictating.

He had worked his way through the pile of correspondence and was about to pass over the catalogue notes when he paused. "That'll be all, Mary," he said. "Send in Miss Murphy, will you?"

Mrs Belman raised an eyebrow behind her hornrims. One thing about Horace, for all his faults, his pomposity, his garish taste and attempts at high living, he had never been a ladies' man, at least as far as Paxham knew.

Brigit Murphy was a twenty-year-old Irish brunette with a twinkling eye and a figure which divided the sympathies of the office down the middle. The males were all hopefully pro – whatever they said to their wives – and the females hated her guts.

Horace passed Brigit the catalogue notes, rising from his desk and attempting an avuncular approach.

Brigit's intelligence was directional. Instinct warned her that while Horace might be fairly harmless, any involvement with him was to be avoided. She therefore didn't ask as many questions as would have been adviseable had she considered him more approachable. She knew absolutely nothing about antiques, since her background in Dublin's Rathfarnham had favoured only the plastic and strictly functional.

She pondered for a long time, – anything which might occupy her attention for more than five minutes she found boring – over a silver teapot which to her limited intelligence, appeared to read as being made by "Mister batman". This, she concluded, must be an antiquarian indulgence of infantile taste. So much on that list appeared odd.

That was how a near-classic was compiled. The sale catalogue listed, among other unheard-of rarities, a painting in the French style after 'Whatho', a rare 'Wayne Scott' chair in oak, and wonder of wonder, a teapot by 'Mister Batman'.

Bert's teapot did not receive the publicity it deserved, and misfortune tends to be cumulative.

On Tuesday, first view day, Charlie went down with a violent attack of 'flu.

On the day of the sale Horace Gribble was not feeling very bright either. He usually ate a hearty breakfast before going down to look at the mail. Today he couldn't manage more than a piece of toast.

The sale began at eleven and normally Charlie would have everything ready for him at ten-thirty, the numbered sheets with the reserves marked and any last-minute, special instructions. Bids received by post and 'phone were also Charlie's responsibility, and since no-one in the office seemed to show any intelligent interest in the sale at all, he'd have to deal personally with those as well. Even the arrangement of everything after the view, so that each item could be located as its number was called, had been, to say the least, chaotic.

In Charlie's absence Horace had spent several hours, on the Thursday, looking things over, not at all confidant that the help he had mustered from the Estate Office and in the Town would be able to cope. Unforeseen difficulties might arise. Everything in the hall was certainly numbered correctly and the notations on the catalogue were complete as regards reserves and bids, but Charlie's comments and advice were lacking. Charlie was running a high temperature, and Horace was too concerned with his own health to want to visit him.

He, himself was one of those people who can make themselves feel off colour when faced with difficulties. He felt positively ill this morning. The fact that a carriage clock and a small porcelain figure had been stolen during viewing hours did nothing to improve his mood.

Not every auctioneer is blessed with special skills. A reasonably quick brain will react immediately to the mood of an audience, and this will be reinforced by a familiarity with the goods being sold. A sense of values quickly finds an echo with the bidders. Horace was realising just how important was Charlie's natural sympathy with the market. He wavered in an agony of uncertainty.

As the hall began to fill he felt like an actor about to take the stage in an unfamiliar part without a script. He nodded to one of the regulars, replied vaguely to enquiries about a carpet and a hall table. He felt uncomfortably that everyone knew his quandary. He wished heartily to be somewhere else.

On the rostrum he re-gained a little confidence. The familiar sales books, the two pens, and his grandfather's ivory hammer helped to steady his nerves. He reminded himself of his reputed auction heritage. The fourth generation mustn't let the Firm down – and there was of course, Caligula. A shaft of sunlight struck down through a high window upon the large stone garden figure of a nymph. That was it. Caligula was selling his slaves. He called attention to the Conditions of Sale.

Drawing a deep breath and glancing across at his clerk, he announced the first lot. "Six Victorian chairs, ladies and gentlemen. Hm . . . yes, they look in good condition, ready for your dining room. May I say one hundred, one twenty, one forty? The bidding went on, then faltered. "Are you all finished now at three hundred?" He brought down the hammer at three-hundred and twenty.

Two local housewives bid against each other for a carpet. Eyes flashing, each intent upon ousting her rival, they paid twice the price for the same thing new anywhere in town. The porcelain, tea services and figures, went well, and all to private clients. The bidding came thick and fast, and he offered up a silent prayer that it would so continue. He hadn't clashed with the professionals yet. The bronzes, pictures and silver came later in the sale. He sold the stone figure to the local nurseryman for four-hundred and fifty.

Horace got into the swing of things. He saw fat old Mrs Swinburne, apparently spilling out, garters showing, of an over-stuffed, button-backed chesterfield. "Would you mind standing up, Madam," he joked. "We know it's a comfortable piece but I've got to sell it. No, Sir, the settee, not the lady." The old quip raised the usual tired rustle of appreciation. A long, lanky junk man draped himself over a 'fridge to conceal its excellent condition. He wanted it for home, but the ghosts of a thousand frozen dinners had somehow left a chilling bequest which struck through his thin trousers and gave him cramp in a very awkward place.

And then, just as Horace was settling into a comfortable rhythm, he noticed a gathering of familiar faces. He saw Martin first, the biggest of the local dealers, noticed the shiny bald head. Welford, the silver man from the Coast was near him. Then came Smith of Wellerden, a nearby country town, and he had with him two unfamiliar characters who, from their deliberate country garb, must surely be from London. Mrs Clayton from Hertfordshire completed the group. They chatted loudly enough to warrant a call to order; they were obviously on friendly terms, to Horace ominously so.

The Ring had descended, and Horace, out of sheer nerves, repeated his warning. "Gentlemen, a little less noise, please. If you want to talk please go outside." It didn't improve the atmosphere, merely creating a rustle of protest among the public more distracting than the original disturbance.

When he called the big bronzes which carried a reserve of £200, there was no response at all from the floor. The silence lingered uncomfortably. The private clients looked about. The dealers maintained an outward appearance of complete disinterest.

"Come along now, ladies and gentlemen. These are very fine pieces. Just the thing for your mantelpiece." Since the figures were something over three feet tall there was a spontaneous titter from a little lady at the front who lived in a bed-sitter. "Perhaps not for you, Madam, but I understand these things sell very well in Italy. Come along now. Two hundred I'm bid. May I say two-twenty?"

"Fifty!" Shouted a small, bespectacled man near the door. The group of dealers made no sign at all.

"Fifty-five," said a tentative lady.

"Sixty!" Shouted someone who sensed a bargain.

The bidding crept agonizingly to two-hundred and five pounds. Then Horace, in a sweat of uncertainty, dropped the hammer to the man by the door. Was he fronting for the Ring? Horace wished he knew, but thereafter, just in case, every time the little man raised his catalogue he conjured a few bids out of the air. He hadn't the courage to carry things too far because he wasn't sure of his values. Sellers weren't very understanding. Auctioneers, they imagined, had all the answers. You were supposed to get high prices, but you got blamed if you bought things in.

Horace couldn't quite believe the next entry in his catalogue, and had to look up to see what the porter displayed. "Showin' 'ere, Sir", came the traditional cry. "Lot two 'undred!"

"There appears to have been a typing error, another," floundered the auctioneer, mentally chastising Brigit. "That looks like a silver teapot, a rather nice one I'd say, but I can't sell it as silver unless it's marked, of course. Yes, have a look at it madame. I'm sure there aren't any holes in it. It'll make a good cup of tea.

"Now what am I bid for this rather nice-er, Batman teapot?"

There came a rustle among the audience. The old hands heard the ribald whispers and knew that the auctioneer was lost.

"One pound!" called a hopeful.

"Two."

Trying to look as if he recognized a new bidder Horace began to take imaginery calls from the door marked "Gentlemen". The little man with the glasses followed his gaze and knew there was no-one there. "Twenty pounds!" And then, when Horace countered with "Twenty-two", he raised his catalogue high.

"Could you show me whom I'm bidding against, Sir?"

He made no further protest when Horace said "twenty-three" and brought the hammer down.

Horace had been so absorbed in his exchange with the phantom bidder that he entirely failed to notice the blue-suited, gesticulating figure in the far corner of the hall, over by the makeshift canteen, where the W.I. dispensed refreshment for the benefit of their funds. By now he really had worked up a temperature. His glasses were steaming over.

# Typical Teapot

Horace sighed with relief as he knocked down the last lot, a brass-bound mahogany writing box. He sold it to an earnest young gentleman with spectacles for the opening bid of fifty pence. Nobody else was interested. The Ring group had moved elsewhere. The buyers were all intent to mark a place in the payment queue.

The young man, standing just below the rostrum, had bought nothing else. He worked in Paxham library. Horace knew him. He gave the porter fifty pence and a five pence tip, for he was a careful young man with imminent matrimonial prospects. Carrying his purchase with both hands carefully before him he emerged into the late afternoon sunshine.

The Green beckoned. There was a mellow rustic seat from which the older inhabitants were wont to be very wise about village cricket matches. There had been a bench on that spot for a century and more. The oak tree which had sheltered it was commemorated by a stump of immense breadth. In the old days it was the ambition of every young buck to score a six by hitting the oak. Sixes were infrequent in these days of strategic play, but occasionally a grounded four did strike the stump and bounce high in the air as if in memoriam to more robust times.

The young man sat down and placed the box on his knees before him. It was a nice box, he decided. He would polish it up on Sunday. He lifted the lid; apart from a writing slope and two ink bottles it appeared to be empty. Then he noticed the button on the back edge. He tried to remove it; it was untidy, and as he pulled, a long depressed spring was released. A concealed drawer shot forward and a bundle of papers fell onto the grass.

They were tied together with what appeared to be old red Admiralty tape. Writing covered them, a solidly formed calligraphy not entirely even. A schoolboy? No. This may have been a young fist but no schoolboy wrote it. The young man forgot time, place, everything, even the date with his fiancee. He read:

23rd August 1800
Colchester Barracks

Charles Graves Esquire,
Clayburne Hall,
Paxham,
Kent.

Dear Mr Graves,

I apologize that I am only now discovering the leisure and the inclination to write telling you of my adventures.

Firstly my time has been fully occupied, and I must admit to a great feeling of homesickness when I write, for then I cannot but think upon the many kindnesses I have received from you all and the good times we have spent together. So I must beg you to present my most respectful greetings to my Patron and Richard, to Mistress Briggs and Masters Crackett and Porter, and of course any other you in your wisdom believe I should remember. You see how well I hold you in regard now that I have had opportunity to apply your good instruction in the great world beyond Paxham!

No doubt you will read this over the tea dishes and the typical teapot. I see you in my mind's eye, you, Richard and His Lordship, who I hope is now in good spirits and fully recovered from the indisposition under which he laboured at my departure.

My Colchester arrival, I must tell you, was not as I expected. It was in this wise.

I found the barracks without much ado, albeit I was still somewhat heavy-eyed from travelling through the night. My travelling companions on either side were two buxom matrons returning home from a domestic excursion who talked without ceasing. They kept out the chill of the night but sleep was difficult in their company.

At last I descended, and at the guard house handed Lord Clayburne's letter to a soldier. After a considerable wait I was paraded to the Colonel.

From the Colonel, after another delay during which my heart, beating high at the thought of my forthcoming adventures, fell to the region of my midriff, I was shuffled off to the Adjutant. From the Adjutant I went to the Serjeant Major while it fell further still, and thence to the Drum Major. My heart had fallen to my new boots by the time I had reached the Drum Major's wife, a drunken Irish woman with whom I must admit to a great feeling of loneliness even though about twenty other boys had gathered to watch my arrival and poke fun at my fine clothes.

But Maggy, for that was the Irish woman's name, soon sent them scattering by throwing a heavy stick at their heads, and then, bidding me sit beside her, asked if I had any pence. I handed her a shilling which I fortunately had apart from the two crowns I had received from His Lordship. This, I soon learned, was far too generous, for she swept off, to return a short while after with only two pies and no change, it being obvious from the unsteadiness of her gait that most of the money had fallen into the pot-man's pocket.

The following morning my head was shaved, with the exception of a small patch of the long hair behind. Then I was paraded to the tailor's shop, where in exchange for my new clothes (which I had but three days and was now supposed to sell) I was served with red jacket and weskitt, pantaloons and forage cap. These garments sat so ill upon me that I felt like a scarecrow and was forced to run a file-fire of hoots and catcalls and cries of "Johnny Raw", as I made my way back to the barracks.

Now among the loudest of those who jeered and pointed was one who stood a full head above his companions. I had heard him called "Jeb" by his cronies and noted how, with knowing winks and nudges he contrived to aggravate my situation. There seemed but one response for Master Jeb, and when I could stomach his jibes no further, and bearing in mind your counsel of prudence before attack, I at last, in spite of my flapping attire, took his arm in the hold you have demonstrated to us and fetched him up in a bucket of slops by the barrack wall. Having demonstrated that I was no coward I am treated now with a certain measure of respect.

That same evening I underwent the operation of having my hair tied up for the first time, to the no small amusement of my colleagues. A large piece of candlegrease was applied, first to the sides of my head, then to the long hair behind. After this the operation was repeated with a nasty, stinking soap. Then a pad filled with sand was poked into the back of my head round which the hair was gathered tight and the whole tied with a leather thong. When an enormous stock had been pushed under my chin I felt as if I had swallowed a ramrod, for I could scarcely close my eyes, and when I attempted to eat, my pad went up and down on the back of my head like a sledge-hammer.

I did not see the Colonel again until the following day when the Serjeant Major paraded us. Observing my somewhat over-large attire he stroked his chin and remarked that my military bearing was to be commended. He then lifted the shoulders of my jacket, demonstrating that whereas I stood stiff as a pikestaff my clothing refused to do likewise.

Back to the tailor then I was despatched for matters to be amended, and at that moment, to my great delight, up stepped the Master of the Band to request my removal to the band room for instruction on the flute and triangle.

So I now have fitting attire and learn the flute. There is much work to be done about the camp, but I believe that I shall do well enough at soldiering.

My respects to Lord Clayburne and Master Richard and all my friends.

Your Ob't Servant William Fibb.

The young man raised his eyes and looked about. The activity at the saleroom continued. Furniture was loading into trucks and onto car racks. Two village ladies trundled past pretending not to see the man from the library, bearing like the workmen in the old paint advertisement, a long, rolled carpet. A tinkle and a loud gasp from somewhere out of sight signalled the dropping of porcelain or glass. People emerged, shouted comments, went on their way. The young man looked at his watch, wondered if he should proceed yet to his rendez-vous. The watch, he remembered, was fast. He selected another of his papers.

Colchester Barracks
3rd March 1801

Charles Graves Esq.,
Clayburne Hall,
Paxham.

Dear Mr Graves,

For two whole weeks I have been unable to continue the relation of my affairs but let me first make amends by expressing my sincere hope that all is well at Clayburne and that my esteemed Patron is by now improved in health. You related the purchase of the pair of steppers for the carriage and that Richard has taken them in hand. Is his skill much increased? And how fare the new fan tails for the pigeon loft? They must look very pretty parading by the yew hedge where, as you must remember, I shed the potato which was to be Mrs Pennyfeather. How the time passes!

My own career, I am pleased to tell you, prospers well in the military line, and I beg you to address your next communication – that is, of course, providing you consider me worthy of a few lines – to Fife Major William Fibb. Does that not sound grand? It came about in this wise.

The flute presented no great difficulties since the skill of one's fingers on such a small instrument, providing, of course, that the breathing is sound, soon takes the rhythm of marching and there is elation in keeping the beat of the drum. Of more concern to me was my poor triangle, which, in keeping the measure, I beat so thin that it was like to fall apart.

My musical bent has saved me many arduous duties in the cleaning and slopping out line, and one of the officers, a Lieutenant Broadbent, has taken kindly to my enthusiasm, so I fondly thought that only pleasant prospects lay in the future. But I had cause for great apprehension some weeks ago when there suddenly arrived a number of volunteers from the militia which included several flute players. The musicians were now so swollen in numbers that I feared for my position.

But Fortune has continued to smile upon me.

At the suggestion of Lieutenant Broadbent and the Bandmaster I have for some time been put to the fife, a circumstance which stood me in good stead in the new band. My new office is no small one, I do assure you.

I have thrown off my red parade coat, and for it have a splendid white jacket with silver lace and epaulette and a tremendous sash which touches almost to the ground. Twice a day we beat through the streets when the weather is fine, followed sometimes by half the boys and girls in the Town.

I thank you for the garments knitted by Mrs Crackett and best wishes from the Parson. I await with interest some news of how the Paxham men fared in the cricket at Bromley and look forward to an opportunity to return home for a few days. Is there any prospect of you and Richard visiting Colchester? It is a fine place.

His Lordship's consideration in the matter of the increased allowance is greatly appreciated and I doubt not you had some influence in the affair. Mr Prothero's agent in the Town is very helpful. My very sincere best regards to all my friends at Clayburne.

Yr. Obed't Servant, William Fibb

He read on. Old script fades and one cannot read it fast. The adventures of a young boy, then a young man, gripped him across the years. The bustle around the old village hall died away then revived as a group of strangers argued and gesticulated as if involved in an esoteric rite. Then they too were gone. As the evening chill crept across the grass the young man looked at his watch again.

He was a full hour late for his appointment.

He had never been an ardent swain. The young woman who worked in a bank had made the running. Books now, they were different; books and reading, finding out and studying. Original information; his box was full of it. He returned his papers to the drawer and hurried back to his bedsitter in the Victorian street which survived behind the new estate.

In his room he brewed a pot of tea. He was old enough to dislike tea bags. One of his few conceits was the possession of a very fine caddy spoon, and as he followed his grandmother's ritual of one for himself and one for the pot, he remembered a line in the first of his letters. "The typical teapot". He wondered about it as he sipped his strong sweet tea and munched his corned beef sandwich.

He took out the letters, opened a fold of lined foolscap paper on the table, and as he read far into the night, he made notes. Then he began his own paraphrase. Perhaps there was material here for a book of his own.

* * *

In the month of August, 1803, Fife Major Fibb, a lusty lad of fifteen summers, fifed his way on the heels of the Drum Major, at the head of a travel-worn file of regulars and recruits into the barracks at Hilsea, overlooking Portsmouth. Beneath him the houses straggled down to the water. The masts and spires of England's ships, great and small, were crowded together, thick as kidney-bean sticks, at the quays, all the way up to Spithead.

William, a seasoned campaigner now, often sat on the Portsdown Hills dreaming of the magical places to which he would soon be sailing in one of the great ships below. He mentioned, several times, in correspondence with his old tutor, that "without doubt he would shortly be for Overseas".

Portsmouth, at that time, presented a picture of great colour and animation. Soldiers from most of the great regiments came there, sailors in their thousands. The blue, white and purple of the Royal Dock ropewalkers struck contrast with the scarlet and blue of artillery and infantry. The boy volunteers were known as the Red Knights, and on a summer's day the sound of fife and drum set many a foot a-tapping. William saluted the great Lord Nelson himself as he strutted out of the Old George. He saw John Pounds, the dockyard worker, who, having sustained injury at his regular trade, turned his hand to shoe-making and the instruction of poor children. He wrote of a fight in a tavern over a doxy, in which perished Jeb, he whom he had thrown into the slops at Colchester.

It was a full year before he crossed any water at all, and his vessel was no Argo, his voyage no Argosy. He embarked near the head of his file on a small naval sloop bound for Jersey at four, one afternoon.

Nevertheless, with head high at the thought of the wide world of adventure just below the horizon he paraded the deck, cane under arm like a seasoned campaigner. Legs apart, steady against the gentle, pleasant swaying of the deck in harbour, he observed the sailors at windlass and line with a knowing look as if he had done it all before. He must have thrilled to the spirit of the age as the vessel edged, creaking, into the fairway with every rope stretched, sails swelling to the eager wind as the small gathering of relatives on the wharf raised a sporadic cheer.

Alas for the calm and uneventful departure, for the heavens opened when they were but an hour on the way. Then the wind rose, and rain fell in sheets. When the thunder crashed upon the unready company the ship's crew made haste to batten down the hatches.

The Military shouted, children squalled, sailors swore, and all the while the wind continued to rise. William revelled in the chaos. He had squeezed himself into a small compass near the helm and was braced against a windlass when a freak wave broke over the ship and carried away the forestaysail. William's own hand best conjured back the military urgency of the day.

"At that moment a sailor cried 'Light ahead!' At which the Captain, who was on the bridge near him, joked, 'Frenchman, I suppose!' The word was at once taken up by one of our military officers who still, by some miracle, contrived to stay upon deck, it being, I think, like mine, his first campaign.

"Strutting valiantly, with some loss of dignity due to the steepness of the deck, he took up the cry.

" 'A Frenchman! Muster the Men! Serjeant, the Bugler! Sound to Arms! Call the Drummer! Beat to Arms!'

"But devil a Serjeant, drummer, drums, bugle or bugler was forthcoming. In the meantime another great sea swept upon us and took away the noble captain's cocked hat, which disconcerted him so much that the strange light had faded to leeward long before he was again in marching order."

On the Island of Jersey William first discovered that Eve had more to offer than an apple.

* * *

The young man from the library detected a break in the tempo of the correspondence with Mr Graves. The phrases were suddenly formal and there were descriptions of sunsets and things abstract. There was mention of a certain General Summers. The young man, like many whose personal amatory ambitions lacked zest, was capable of considerable vicarious imagination. Under the bundle of letters he found a diary. The boyish writing had become firm. It was small and even. He began to consider the creation of a romance, a history of William Fibb.

* * *

Once, as William, with the day's duty behind him, sauntered along the beach, he observed the passing of a comely young woman in a blue gown. That evening, instead of making a note for his erstwhile tutor he wrote three verses. For several days, from ravally to taptoo, his eye had a vacant look and twice he missed his step on the march.

On Sunday afternoon, still wearing his best regimentals from morning church parade (they made him look older than his years) William was walking along a secluded part of the sands when he heard a light gasp from behind a rock. Creeping up to investigate he found himself regarding the object of his sonnets, blue gown and all, though in a state of disarray, and prostrate upon the ground.

"Begging your pardon, Mistress," was all he could stammer as he turned to flee, but she stayed him with a gesture, and he noticed that her cheek, though blooming, was stained by a tear.

"Oh, please don't go away, Sir – I believe I have twisted my ankle!"

"What would you have me do, Ma'am . . . Mistress,' blushed William. "Must you go far?"

"Only to the top of the beach, Sir, up there," she replied, pointing to an imposing mansion some two hundred yards away. "If you would kindly lend me your arm."

Very formal and soldier-like he proferred a military elbow, but the ankle was painful.

"There's but one thing for it," eyelashes fluttering to the confusion of the gallant soldier. "You'll have to carry me!"

From the corner of his eye, William could see two companions approaching. He was very stiff and polite. He took out his kerchief, dipped it in a rocky pool and stooped to bind the offending member.

"Perhaps," he said, "that will ease the hurt. Would you oblige by telling me your name?"

"Oh, I'm Miss Summers; they call me Caroline. "How do they call you?"

"Fibb," said William. "Fife Major Fibb; they call me Will."

"My father's a General," said Caroline, with a directness which almost precipitated a panic retreat by the Fife Major. "But don't worry. He's nice really, and he's retired in any case. Come along now. You'll just have to carry me home!"

Caroline was of a rounded disposition and she made an awkward burden. William, in his efforts to preserve the proprieties and his military bearing at the same time, gave her a rough passage. She tried to help him during the latter part of the journey, by throwing a plump arm round his neck, but since he was thus almost smothered by her draperies progress was confused.

She was a kindly young person. As they approached the front door she kissed her rescuer full on the lips.

Thus the encounter between the Fife Major and the General's daughter was double confounded.

As they reached the front door, Mrs Summers met them. It was a double door, but none thought to open the half which was bolted. In the narrow opening Mrs Summers tried to be helpful. She pushed and pulled. Meanwhile a maid, approaching from the garden, pulled and pushed, and at last William, beneath the weight of all three, collapsed, half in and half out of the house, his shako over his eyes, nearly stifled by an ample bosom – whose, he knew not.

With difficulty he raised a veil of draperies, provoking a chorus of coy screams as he did so, perceiving, to his horror, through what appeared to be a forest of stockinged ankles, the approach of an elegantly dressed, small round gentleman waving a broadsheet, crying "Mrs Summers! Mrs Summers! Tippoo's dead!"

The General disentangled his womenfolk, and having established the innocuous origins of the apparent assault, invited William to stay for a dish of tea.

Caroline reclined upon a silken couch. The General said his eldest son was in India where the notorious Tippoo Sahib had been cornered at Seringapatam.

William remarked gravely that he hoped Lieutenant Summers would have survived the action with credit, and casting a languishing eye upon his erstwhile burden, thought first of a line for a new sonnet and then added that he wished that he too would one day visit India, although he had heard that being an Officer, a distinction he had every intention to achieve, in that quarter, was reserved, he thought, only for those employed by the East India Company.

It was perhaps, just as well that shortly afterwards, Fife Major William Fibb returned to Hilsea.

* * *

The young man found the Fibb letters absorbing. Next day he again missed an assignment with his inamorata.

The following evening, as he went about his rather elementary preparations for cooking supper, a knock on his door introduced his landlady. She, in turn, with a haughty sniff, grudgingly stepped aside to permit the entry of his fiancée. Paxham was very parochial and she left muttering direly about "not staying too late".

The romance hitherto had drifted. He was what an Army man might have described as lacking in initiative. She, on the other hand, knew exactly what she wanted, and so far in her young life, most things had come fairly easily.

She would stay working at her bank, marry and have a family, and the young man at the library, for reasons emotionally obscure, as are so many affairs of the heart, should be her chosen mate.

But now he had defaulted – twice!

"Darling," she said as soon as the door closed on the landlady. "We've got to talk things over."

The landlady's dictat was forgotten, and there wasn't much in the way of conversation.

When they went out after breakfast, to a twitching of curtains at the windows of neighbouring houses, she to the bank and he to his library, where his work that day lacked something of its customary efficiency, a wedding had been arranged. He was a prim and proper young man, some would have called him old-fashioned. When that kind of thing happened, well, you just had to marry the girl; and he was really quite pleased about it.

The only information added to the Fibb saga came not from the cache of letters at all. The verger found some notes which a nineteenth century predecessor had compiled and left in one of the old locked bookcases in the vestry. They only came to light when an ancient two-volume Concordance was being thrown out by the Vicar. The Verger took the notes to the library in case they might be of use to local historians, and it happened that the young man was on duty at the time.

The Verger was surprised and gratified at the interest shown in his discovery. As he said to his wife that evening over the fish and chips he took home once a week to give her a bit of a rest with her arthritic fingers. "Odd, they were, something about Maida Vale."

"Yes," she said, harking back to her youth. "Went there once, right at the top of the Edgware Road."

"You just don't know what young people'll be interested in nowadays. The Vicar says it'll be alright for the library to take a copy. Then we won't have to bother the P.C.C."

The notes put flesh upon the bones provided by William Fibb's oddly endearing, formally phrased, letters home. A contemporary observer's comment brought new perspective. The young man read the notes thoroughly before putting them away with the letters.

*Battle of Maida 1806. Engraving by A. Cardon after F.J. de Loutherbourg. Published 1810.*

Ensign William Fibb went to Italy, and after a colourful sequence of meanderings in the Calabrian Hills with Lieutenant, later Captain, Clayburne among brigands and larger-than-life Countesses, he fought beside him at the Battle of Maida. That curious action was said to have been suspended while an eccentric British sporting peer led his mounted colleagues and the pack of hounds he had brought with him on the campaign, down between the opposing lines, in pursuit of a fox!

William married a Calabrian beauty named Bella and returned eventually to Clayburne as Manager of the family Estate, a wound having put paid to his military aspirations. He did much to alleviate the circumstances of the unfortunates at the Orphanage, and one of his first cares, on his return home, was the banishment of the ageing Pennyfeathers.

William and Bella had one son, and after her husband's death from a fever she yielded to his manifestation of the family wanderlust. Bella and her son emigrated to America.

What appeared to the young man as a curious irrelevance came at the bottom of the second page of the vestry notes.

" 'When he went he took with him the 'typical' Clayburne silver tea service left to him by his father."

The young man from the library and the young lady from the bank almost forgot the box of letters in the attic. She mentioned them occasionally in terms of "clearing out the rubbish" to make an extra room with a dormer window directly beneath the roof, but that would be costly and only necessary if, well, if she could leave the bank for a while to raise a family.

History, in the way of things, must give way to the present. For the time being the owners of the letters had other things to occupy their minds.

# Boston Teapot

It was a large envelope with a bank-like logo on one corner. A pretentious "Gribble, Funnel and Duck" filled in the space until you reached a red inked square with a caption advising immediate attendance at the next Fine Art Sale. It didn't impress Bert.

He leafed hurriedly through the catalogue to see how the items were sectioned off. Pictures, furniture and porcelain, he found all those, but there wasn't any silver heading. There wasn't anything he recognised under "Miscellaneous Items" either.

So he sat down on one of his oddly situated armchairs in the bathroom, and meticulously checked every item in the sale. There were three teapots. One was with two odd candlesticks and was possibly "Beleek" but unmarked. The second one was copper, Tibetan and a foot high. The third was a silver teapot alright, but it was called "Mister Batman" so Bert assumed it must be some child's affair, out of a nursery. Perhaps Charlie had decided this sale wasn't suitable and held the pot over, but in that case why had he sent the catalogue?

Against all his natural instincts Bert decided to make a telephone call. He hated all things mechanical, hadn't used a coin box in years, but this was a matter of urgency. He selected a number of coins against the contingency of immense charges, and with his pocket weighed down made his way to the 'phone box by the supermarket. It was occupied. A woman could be seen gesticulating into the instrument while two robust youngsters, noses pressed to the glass, whined and grizzled outside. Bert tried to pacify them whereupon the lady put down the receiver, gathered up her bag, spectacle case and small change, and emerged hurriedly.

Bert stood in some surprise as the woman looked suspiciously at him, her offspring setting up a wailing duet as if he had purloined their sweets. Another woman meanwhile entered the telephone box from the far side and settled down for a long cosy chat.

Twenty minutes later Bert dialled the number on the front of the auction catalogue, put ten pence in the slot to cover every possible time and distance factor and was told very curtly that he was through to the estate office and he had better telephone the auction room. No, they didn't think they had a Charlie, not unless he meant the new office boy whose name was Geoffrey and he wasn't allowed telephone calls anyway.

He fished in his pockets for the card Charlie had given him. He'd left it in his best suit. He had to go and fetch it. By the time he finally got through Charlie had gone to lunch. A silver teapot? No, no-one knew anything, about that, unless he wanted to call the estate office and speak to Mr Gribble.

He made one more effort, from another telephone box further up the road, after he'd had his lunch. The number was engaged and apparently remained so during the whole afternoon.

So Bert went back to Paxham for the sale. They wouldn't let him in to see Charlie, and the auctioneer didn't seem to notice his bids.

Cockney obstinacy, native persistence, carried London through the Blitz. Bert knew he had to face an incomprehensible situation on his own. He saw the teapot given away. He noticed that the man bidding was not alone. He waited and watched, and when his quarry left and made his way to "The Coach and Horses", Bert followed; but he was far enough away to allow several other people to enter the bar before he went in himself.

Martin, with a quick glance round out of deference to his Association membership – the Association disapproved of Rings – sat at the head of the long table in the window. He was, after all, senior dealer on his home pitch. He opened his catalogue, took a biro from his pocket and drew columns on the blank tailpiece. Welford sat to his right above Smith and the little man who had stood by the door; they called him Bill. On the other side of the table sat Mrs Clayton and the two men from London. Smith went to fetch a round of drinks.

As he headed up his columns with the initials of his colleagues, none of whom he particularly liked, Martin had time to think about changes in attitudes. He was nearly sixty. He didn't really like messing about with rings. They did constitute a conspiracy to defraud the seller of the full value of his goods. But wasn't it the dealer who was responsible for the creation of value? If he and his friends hadn't been at the sale today would all those old biddies from the village have paid even ten pounds for some of the things which had cost hundreds? In a group of dealers like this, most of whom had been around for years and remembered the old days, what did one do?

Thirty years ago, just after the War, the situation had been regarded differently. In those days auctioneers were just disposers. They knew little about values, and he remembered when old man Funnel who was then mainly concerned with selling cattle, would step from his portable rostrum after a good antique sale and come with the Boys to the local to take his share of the "Knock". Many auctioneers did the same.

Dealers used to be the sole arbiters of value. They studied the few books available, mainly learned theses by lifelong specialists, – now every Tom, Dick and Harry put pen to paper – watched the old hands, looked and listened. They all kept quiet about what they knew, didn't shout it from the housetops, wising the mugs!

The conferring of Chairmanship of the Ring had then been a mark of respect to the senior member present in any group of dealers. They regarded themselves as a cut above common or garden businessmen. Other Professionals, like solicitors, doctors, even insurance-men came to them for advice.

Nowadays the value of most things was common knowledge and the outlook had to be different. Here was Smith with his pint. Martin shrugged his shoulders and hoped that nobody who mattered was watching. Hopes are seldom realised.

Bert, leaning awkwardly on the bar over a pint of bitter, had already decided that he wouldn't give a dollar for the gleaming lacquered copper fakes which glinted from every nook and cranny of the harsh fibre-glass oak. He heard Martin offer the bronzes. "They cost two-hundred and five quid. To save time I'll put on fifty." One of the London men held them for seven-fifty.

"Not bad", reflected Martin. "Five-forty-five in the kitty and there's only seven of us." There was going to be a windfall, particularly for those who hadn't intended to hold goods anyway.

The next lot was a small ship model under a glass dome. It was fashioned of bone, and Horace had made great play of his little knowledge of the French Prisoners of War at Norman Cross. Martin, out of his years of experience, produced a memory. He knew that particular type of model. He'd examined that specimen carefully. The tiny cannon, which should have been of brass or hardwood, were an indeterminate light brown in colour, made, he knew of spaghetti, by a curious little Italian faker in the forties. Quite a character he'd been; knew more about ships than most sailors. Martin looked round the circle. The boat had been bought for a hundred, already, he considered, fifty pounds more than it was worth.

One of the Londoners thought he knew better. Over eight-hundred pounds were added to the kitty.

Brigit's catalogue produced several more bargains, each of which added its quota to the already considerable sums accumulating in Martin's catalogue.

At last he came to the teapot. "Twenty-three we paid for that. Batman's best – wonder what Robin would have thought of it? Thank the Lord for this world's Horaces. Don't know how they get away with it. "I'll go fifty again."

"One hundred." "One fifty," Two hundred", "Two fifty", "three fifty, "Four hundred." It was back to Martin, and he wished he hadn't started so high. Four-fifty was one-fifty above his pessimistic maximum, and he almost withdrew. But he felt that he had to defend his home patch. "Four-fifty", he said nonchalantly and looked to Welford. But no-one advanced the bidding. The second man from London breathed a sigh of relief. He hadn't wanted the thing anyway. It couldn't be "right" with that curious finial. Teach these country bumkins a lesson.

It took half an hour and another round of drinks to organise the settlement. There was a lot to count and some hadn't brought sufficient cash, but there was a good day's work for everyone.

Bert had finished his pint and gone long before the party strayed back across the green, and Martin, having been delayed by a stranger, hurried to tail the queue for payment and collection.

Bert was not the only one to observe the knockout.

Gerald Ponsonby-Smollett who spoke with a public school plum in his mouth and liked to pretend that his accent was actually the birth mark of a silver spoon, came from Peckham. Ineffective at most things, he started an antiques business on the proceeds of a small legacy from a doting aunt.

Six months had been sufficient to reduce his capital to a shadow. Gerald thought he had flair, sharing the common misconception that a few books and a little knowledge are the key to a fortune in the art world. They can be, if you're exceedingly lucky. Most antique dealers, if they survive, are grateful to providence, and many, the wise ones, after a lifetime, confess that they still know nothing.

How much was there to know about a simple teapot? To those in the Ring it was just another item among the Trade ephemera, an unusual pot with a maker's and a date mark. It was to be bought at one price and sold, hopefully, at another. Who thought for one moment that it was made to the crowd's acclaim at Lunardi's ascent, had seen a young lad's grooming for a war in Italy, crossed the Atlantic and returned in a Chinese junk, been in a pawnbrokers on Brixton Hill, suffered burglary and blitz, and returned to its home village to have the dents restored by a Japanese brainwave?

Gerald Ponsonby-Smollett hadn't a clue. He had read in a book about

Hester Bateman's mark and remembered that she was dismissed casually as being merely the firm's bookkeeper.

He didn't know about price, and the morning's interview with his bank manager made him care even less. Unless funds were paid in on the morrow outstanding cheques would not he honoured.

Gerald was a poseur to the last.

Martin did not regard himself as an ultimate expert. He made no claims to connoisseurship and his opinion of what he regarded as the modern breed of know-all armed with a price-guide, could be expressed in vitriolic terms. But he had been around for a long time and he had an instinctive sense of value. The teapot, he felt, was a mistake. He had paid too much, and he didn't like off-setting his knock-money against silly bids. He had seen Gerald at other sales and had never thought him worthy of consideration among the knockout boys.

He was surprised, even delighted, when he came up. "Mr Martin, I'm Gerald Ponsonby-Smollett. Would you consider a small profit?"

"I'm afraid, Mr – what did you say your name was?"

"Gerald'll do."

"Well, Gerald, I'm afraid it's cost a little more now than twenty-three pounds."

"I know. I was watching."

An awful thought occurred to Martin.

"Er, you're not on one of the newspapers?"

Gerald suppressed a smile. "No, I've a shop in Walton.

Martin breathed a sigh of relief. "Twenty-five profit okay?", and Gerald Ponsonby-Smollett, reasoning that what Martin bought for four hundred and fifty must be worth considerably more, quickly wrote out a worthless cheque for four hundred and seventy-five pounds.

Everyone was happy. A good day and plenty of spare cash.

Martin wrote out a cheque and lined up the purchases as he collected them by the tailboard of his shooting brake.

The stand-in porter, one of Horace Gribble's office clerks who had boasted for years that he could do Charlie's job on his head, was learning a thing or two. Now he was getting hot under the collar. People kept enquiring about transport, wanted boxes and paper, asked questions to which he didn't know the answers; and now he couldn't find the bloody teapot.

He looked everywhere. He asked everyone. At last he called a nervous and feverish Horace, who couldn't find it either. Horace expressed regrets; and when the man with the glasses actually threatened violence he merely handed over a cheque for twenty-three pounds. When it came to the crunch, the Ring were hoist with their own petard. They couldn't complain too loudly without disclosing their illegal interest. And Martin had noticed the reporter from the Paxham Cornet hovering for tit-bits of scandal.

Gerald Ponsonby-Smollett took back his cheque; Martin seethed; Smith and Welford stood consoling Mrs Clayton; the men from London remained aloof until the reverse knock had been organised. Money, once it has been distributed, is not easy to recoup. Those who hadn't wanted the pot in any case were now desolate at its disappearance, and it took a long time to work out, since Martin couldn't find his notes, who had to refund how much to whom.

Charlie heard about the affair when he got up two days later. He didn't know how to break the news to Bert, nor did he know about his visit. He wasn't well enough to go chasing up to Battersea either, but he didn't seem over-concerned. Years spent in the turmoil of an auction room tend to encourage the philosophical approach.

* * *

Anthony Godfrey didn't look at all like his name. Not surprising, really, since his father years ago had insisted that to give himself a better chance in life he should cease to be Aby Gottfried. Well, what's in a name? When the new Anthony moved to a posh district his friends promptly dubbed him Aby all over again, and Aby he'd remained ever since.

He sat in his Chelsea shop among a stock of glittering silver, silver plate and jewellery. It was a large stock in a small shop. Aby was small too, small and round like a Queen Anne bullet teapot with spectacles. He was looking at two small silver items, a cream jug and sugar box, and he'd just established their date as 1784. Hester Bateman too. Untypical shape they were, which was why they'd been in the window all weekend without anyone noticing.

Another rotund figure tapped at the locked glass door. You had to be careful now, with all the hold-ups, specially with goods like silver – but this was Solly Goldstein wanting to come in. Aby pressed the release button down behind the glass counter.

The badly-connected door bell buzzed Solly over the threshold with a metallic stutter.

'Vell, Aby," he said, "vot bargains you got today?"

"Solly, my friend. All my stock is bargains. Tell you what I do. I bought the Hester Bateman cream jug and bowl for two hundred only last week. Two twenty-five and its' yours!"

Solly knew his friend had only paid one fifty, but he kept up the charade. "Vot I vant with a cream jug and basin? If you had, for instance, a teapot to go with I might offer."

"I should be so lucky," said Aby, and that was when Bert tapped on the door.

He had discovered that a Hester Bateman teapot was not always the easiest of sellers. When he brought it back to town he was full of high hopes. He knew how the Ring had reckoned it, saw the price at which the hammer fell, and guessed rightly that such a small theft would not appear on the lists of stolen goods.

But when he overcame his London Saleroom inhibition and presented himself at the counter of the biggest establishment he could think of – in his best suit, of course – his worst fears were realised. It was like being in Church. He found himself between a fat Polish Countess and a Guards Officer in mufti, and the young female, very well spoken and polite behind pebble spectacles, was not encouraging. "Oh yes, sir, I'll certainly have our expert look at it, but I don't really think it would be worth our while selling a Sheffield plated teapot on its own." The Guards Officer was clamouring to see the Earl of Somewhere who was on the Board, so Bert picked up his teapot, wrapped it deliberately in a large red handkerchief, and left.

He tried two shops after that. In the first a young gentleman of immaculate diction and person told him with a barbed smile, "Sorry, sir. We don't buy from casual callers."

In the next shop, a hopeful secretary, with an eye to breaking away and setting up a market stall on her own account instead of making a fortune for a skinflint boss, offered him all that was left of her wages, six pounds.

Once more he tried, and an elderly gentleman with a bald head asked him point blank if it was "nicked". Bert assumed a cherubic expression of outraged dignity, whereupon the man, producing an eye-glass with the sleight of hand born of very long practice, examined the hallmark. "Hm – HB eh? Hester Bateman? Must be a fake. That's never a piece of Bateman silver – wrong shape. Try Sotheby's."

On the Sunday, he walked down from Notting Hill Gate, idly speculating on the possibilities of a new "beat", and there, in a silversmith's window, he noticed a jug and basin. The basin had a lid, which was unusual.

Aby looked at Solly who shook his head. They took no notice. Bert knocked again. Then he held up his teapot. Aby pressed the button. After all, Solly was there to help in the event of trouble.

"Would you buy a silver teapot, Mister?" said Bert tentatively.

"Look mate," said Aby, "I got a straight business here, all up and above board. Don't want no bent gear, understand? How much you wanting for your teapot?"

"Three-fifty," said Bert, with a sheepish grin.

"Mishugge," said Solly.

"Tell you what," said Aby, "You prove you come by that teapot honest an' I'll give you two hundred."

"I'll prove it's straight," said Bert, "but I ain't takin' no two 'undred. Three-fifty or I'm orf." He turned to the door.

"Take a cheque?" queried Aby, "Two-fifty, but you've got to prove who you are and where you got it."

"No cheques," said Bert. "Ain't got no bank account."

Eventually Bert produced a grubby card from Gribble, Funnel and Duck and suggested that Aby should ring up Charlie and ask if he knew Bert. He hoped his friend was better.

Aby got Charlie on the line after a short delay. Charlie's comments were obviously satisfactory because Aby passed the telephone to Bert immediately after he'd spoken.

Bert put the instrument to his ear as if it was hot.

"That you, Bert?" He heard Charlie chuckle. "You old devil. Haven't changed much, 'ave you? I guessed you managed to look after yourself. Ought to be shot, they ought, Ringing you like that. Get a good price, mate, if only for old times' sake." Then came a pause. "Bert . . ."

"Yes, Charlie?"

"Look, mate. I don't want you to worry 'bout me, see. I insured that teapot for two hundred pounds in my own name. Got a friend in the business. Just makes up nicely for the perks I didn't get with missing the sale. Thanks, chum . . . come and stay down here when you've got time. Cheerio!"

Bert finally got three hundred pounds cash for his teapot. A good price. But Aby sold the three pieces to Solly for six hundred, also in cash, so everyone – almost – really did rather well.

* * *

A Friday afternoon in 1975. A gentleman with a slight limp, and a lady who, if asked, would have called herself middle-aged, were sauntering down Bond Street. She held fast to his arm and there was an air of companionable content about them. Here were two people who, having weathered the hazards of youth, had lived well, and now contemplated the future without apprehension.

Outside a silversmith's, the couple stopped. "Look, Jan," said the man,

*A stock of silver in Bond Street today.*

"look at that tea set. Isn't it like the one they gave us at Huxley. Remember that?"

"Yes," said Janet Ashley, squeezing his arm. "I remember. But this one must be special. It's marked . . . a thousand, is it? . . . can't see the ticket. No, it's fifteen hundred pounds!"

As they moved away down the street, two elegant hands, snowy cuffed and heavily gold-linked, carefully gathered up the three pieces from behind the iron grille.

In the shop, in a reproduction Chippendale armchair, sat a lady of Transatlantic distinction. Very upright in her immaculate black, bediamoned and pearled, she supported two very old and almost transparent ringed hands upon the gold mounting of an eighteenth century major-domo's long stick with a tassle.

The young salesman, with an eye upon his proprietor observing matters discreetly from the glass cubicle of an office at the back of the premises, thought she looked like a monument he'd seen somewhere.

"It's an interesting service, this, Madame. Good shape. Hester Bateman, 1784, well marked. It's the right period for the HB mark, but this does have unusual features. The form is more sophisticated than usual – and look at those cast finials." He was getting into his stride. The nearer the sale approached the ticket price the greater his commission. This tea set wasn't an easy seller. Things which didn't entirely conform to traditional style often weren't. The old lady said nothing. He thought he knew her, she'd been in before; what was her name?

Mrs Lambert, that was it; Mrs George Lambert Junior. She came from Boston. He turned the teapot so that a ray of sunlight made it glitter.

"It really is elegant, Mrs Lambert, don't you think? Look at that delicate bright-cutting, just like lace. Unfortunately, we haven't been able to identify the crest. It's too worn, but it probably came from a noble house." He eyed the customer, rightly sized her up. "It looks feminine somehow, . . . er . . . experienced."

Mrs Lambert raised a gold lorgnette. "Young man," she boomed, in a cracked falsetto, "you're a good salesman, but feminine? Experienced?"

She upturned the pot and inspected the base.

"You see those scratches? That's a pawn mark. I'd have described it as well-used and mellow!" Her eyes twinkled like an old-cut diamond with the ghost of a smile. The young man wondered if that had been a joke.

"It's a good tea-set; a bit expensive, but you can't have everything. Make it fourteen hundred and I'll take it."

A discreet nod was observable from the glass cubicle.

"You're getting a bargain, Madame."

"That's as may be, but have it packed and sent by air with the rest of my things. The shippers will send you a cheque."

"Pitt and Scott isn't it, Ma'am?"

"That's right, we've shipped with them for three generations."

With a creak and a rustle she stood up. Then she proceeded through the door held open by the commissionaire to her taxi.

## *A Final Word –for the Moment*

In 1982 Mrs George Lambert Jr. of Boston, Mass. died.

She left her collection of antiques and art works to the City of her birth, with suitable provision for maintenance, hoping that it would provide the foundation of a small museum in memory of her family which had been associated with Boston since the early whaling days.

In the same year the Director of one of the most important Art Foundations in the States fell out with his Board over the purchase of an important classical sculpture, the provenance of which was questioned.

The Director left his Museum to become Editor of one of the most prestigious glossy art magazines. He was an opinionated man who nursed grudges, a fact which became obvious as he commenced, through his writings, to express his views upon the merits of the various collectors, connoisseurs and objects he had known.

Mrs George Lambert, who also had views of her own, was not one of his favourites. Thus it came about that, in a particularly sour editorial, doubt was cast, not only upon her judgement, but also upon the quality and antecedents of many objects in her collection. The passage that dealt with the silver was scathing, with special reference to a service of tea things which "did not in any way conform with accepted standards." In so many words he damned it as not of museum quality.

So the City Fathers, having read the comments of someone who should have known, were more than usually selective. In consultation with the executors they discovered that the terms of Mrs Lambert's will had taken possible refusal of her bequest into account. The acceptable elements of the collection could go, with appropriate acknowledgement, into an existing museum. The remainder, including the tea service, would be put up for auction. The auctioneer entrusted with the disposal was young and very diligent.

With the aid of an ultra-violet lamp, a strong glass and an ancient book on heraldry, he did what no-one had succeeded in doing for over a century and a half. He actually identified the worn crest of Clayburne on the Bateman teapot.

Then he discovered that Paxham had been the seat of the Clayburnes. He went further. He wrote to the librarian at Paxham, Kent, England.

"Good Lord", said the Senior Librarian to his wife. "It seems unlikely, but what a coincidence! That must be the typical teapot!"

"What are you talking about, dear?" said his wife, as he went to fetch the writing box, and the papers, out of the attic.

There could, of course, be more by the day, because, after two hundred years, the tea service shows only minimal surface wear, and a little diminution of the sharpness of the engraving. Otherwise, to all intents and purposes, it's as fresh as it was on the day Hester Bateman handed it to Lord Clayburne.